RUSSIAN ASSAULT

DYLAN REILLY SERIES
BOOK 2

JOHN RUANE

FIRST NOVEL IN DYLAN REILLY THRILLER SERIES

A DANGEROUS FREEDOM

A Dangerous Freedom, an action-packed, fast-paced thriller-novel, introduces Dylan Reilly, the everyman, who never imagined himself owning or using a gun. But after he and his wife are on the site of three deadly attacks, he purchases a Smith & Wesson six-shooter, trains with a former U.S. Marine and becomes incredibly fast with a gun. Then, like a cowboy from the old west with his six-shooter at his side, he confronts armed and dangerous killers carrying semi-automatic weapons. Reilly knows that if he's not lighting fast and deadly accurate innocent people will die.

RAVE REVIEWS

"A Dangerous Freedom is a very fast-paced, action-packed story, which is a mixture of both fact and fiction, emphasizing the importance of patriotism, loyalty and friendship. I was left reeling from the amount of action in this book. At times, Dylan reminded me of a gun-slinger from a western with superhuman ability to take down the bad guys. This story is invigorating from start to finish and had me smiling!"

JENNY DELA CRUZ, ONLINE BOOK CLUB

"A thought-provoking blend of cowboy-style heroism, terrorism inspection, and social commentary that will leave thriller readers thinking long after the final volley is fired."

DIANE DONOVAN, SENIOR REVIEWER, MIDWEST BOOK REVIEWS

"John Ruane has written a compelling story for our times, seen through the lens of Dylan Reilly and a generation coming of age at a time of profound change wrought by globalism, terrorism, fear, and political insecurity. Fast-paced, action-filled, and a moving commentary on war and the state of the post-9/11 world, *A Dangerous Freedom* is a novel with a statement that will be hard to put down."

RICHARD LINDBERG, AUTHOR AND CHICAGO HISTORIAN

★★★★★ **Well Done Thriller**

"Anchored to the events of 9/11, this story takes off and never lets back on the throttle. Intertwining with real-life terrorism, political and social upheavals with the growing realism of terrorism, the author had done a fine job of creating this story. The storyline is more of a modern-day cowboy gunfighter movie, with a reluctant hero that is forced to drop his plow and pick up the gun. I thought about "The Man Who Shot Liberty Valance" on more than one occasion, but in this story, the reluctant hero can shoot well. Great job."

ROLLIN K. MILLER, READER, AMAZON REVIEW

⭐⭐⭐⭐⭐ **One heck of a ride!**

"Almost everyone can recall where they were on 9/11. This book brought me right back to sitting in my 3rd grade classroom with my mother picking me up from school mysteriously early. It ignited a lot of painful memories of that time in my life, but it was cathartic, too. We get to see this event through the eyes of a teenage American boy and watch as his perceptions of those of a certain race are affected and even changed entirely.

This story is so well written, right down to the dialogue. It is engaging, enticing, and kept me on the edge of my seat nearly every chapter. The near death encounters Dylan experiences had my heart racing and tapped into a kind of fear I didn't even know existed. It is real and raw; something most people shy away from. I'll definitely be reading more by this author!"

KRISTINA RYAN, READER, AMAZON REVIEW

⭐⭐⭐⭐⭐ **Action-packed!**

"The inspiring thing about Dylan Reilly is that he will stop at nothing to protect the ones he loves. His character reminds me of Liam Neeson in the "Taken" trilogy, minus all of the professional training, of course. What started out as just an average guy evolved into a gun-toting badass out of pure necessity. This book is a wild ride full of adventure and suspense. A Dangerous Freedom is a one book that you won't want to miss!"

CARISSA, READER, AMAZON REVIEW

RUSSIAN ASSAULT

a thriller

JOHN RUANE

A ROSWELL PRESS BOOK

IBSN: 979-8-9866378-0-8
ISBN (eBook): 979-8-9866378-1-5

Russian Assault
©2022 by John Ruane
All Rights Reserved

Cover art by Nic Ferrari

This book is a work of fiction. Any references to historical events, real people, or real places are used fictitiously. Other people, places, events, and situations are the product of the author's imagination. Any resemblance to actual persons, living or dead, is entirely coincidental.

No part of this book may be reproduced, stored in a retrieval system, or transmitted by any means without the written permission of the author or publisher.

Roswell Press
Roswell, Georgia

To my daughter, Megan, for her ardent support and helpful advice.

CHAPTER ONE

Ken Hack hadn't seen it. But he'd damn well heard it.

There was no mistaking the sound of an RPG being launched. The second he heard the all-too-familiar pop and then the sound of the missile cutting through the night sky, he turned quickly to his right and could see the rocket headed straight at him.

"Incoming!" he yelled into his wrist microphone, dropping to the solid gray metal behind one of the stacks on the roof of the White House. A huge explosion shook the entire building under him. A fireball shot high and far from the Oval Office.

Lying near the ledge, facing south on the roof, he jumped up and sprinted as fast as he could away from the path of the next missile, which he was certain would be directed right at him.

Inside, his Secret Service agents were yelling for everyone to, "Get out!" Fear filled the eyes of staffers as they ran, not knowing where, fires burning in the halls. Away was the destination.

Screams echoed through the halls. The sound of the second RPG-7 pop could be heard.

Hearts raced. Feet flew. The sound of shoes pelted off the carpet. People panicked!

"Run! Run! Run!" yelled someone, somewhere, somehow, in the total chaos.

Above, Hack and his five-man team sprinted toward the far end of the roof over the West Wing, when the missile grenade struck the center of the already-damaged Oval Office. Another thunderous explosion and massive fireball shot out from the heart of the most powerful building in the world.

Hack, the incredibly strong, 6'2" Director of the Secret Service, was sent flying like a human cannonball in a circus. It felt like a bad dream, a nightmare. In the air, he could see his loyal and trusted team members around him. Arms and legs flailing, eyes bulging, mouths screaming. They were like a team of skydivers drifting through the air with no parachutes.

Hack landed hard on his back against the unforgiving roof, bouncing, keeping his head up to avoid a concussion. His shirt sleeves torn, elbows bleeding.

Hack quickly gathered himself. Bumps and bruises wouldn't stop this heroic soldier. He bounced up like a gymnast. His men were scattered across the roof. No time to check them.

He picked up his 300 Winchester Magnum chambered bolt action rifle, ran to the front ledge and aimed toward the smoke cloud billowing from the launch point in The Ellipse, the 52-acre park on the south side of the White House.

Through his binoculars, he could see four men, all dressed in green fatigues. They were hurrying to load another RPG-7, the Russian-made weapon.

Not this time, Hack thought. He had been in this situation many times in Afghanistan, where he had earned the Bronze Star for his courage under fire. He was the best United States Marine Corps sniper in his division, with more than fifty kills. He took great pride in having saved his buddies during a period of the war when soldiers were going door to door, looking for dangerous Taliban fighters. Hack's incredible record had resulted in the White House recruiting him to guard President Gregory H. Walsh and his family.

Over the decade he had roamed the grounds, halls and roof of the White House, he had never had to fire his weapon. It had certainly been locked and loaded the day the misguided flag-draped American man had climbed over the tall, spiked black metal White House fence. Lying on the roof, Hack had his 300 Winchester Magnum pointed at the unwelcome, uninvited intruder, who had raised his arms in victory on the North Lawn. Hack had been relieved to see three heavily armed Secret Service agents and their dogs apprehend the disturbed man, allowing the military veteran to avoid adding another kill to his record.

Despite his rifle's lack of use over that time period, he had never lost the anxiety he felt on a daily basis. He consistently reminded himself and his team of the responsibility they held, protecting the leader of the free world.

The highly trained, muscular, 210-pound patriot knew that it only took one person, one nut, one terrorist to decide to jump that fence with a weapon and a mind full of bad intentions.

Or one cleverly disguised miscreant who outsmarted the security system and passed through the White House E Street security checkpoint.

Or, as he had found out on that evening, four misguided green-fatigued combatants firing two anti-tank RPG-7s at the Oval Office.

And on that hot first day of May in 2015, International Workers' Day, when the dangerous projectile had been fired at the office of the commander-in-chief, President Jack Fallon, the highly determined Ken Hack had no intention of allowing a third shot at the home of a President he loved and admired for his distinguished service as a naval aviator, who had been shot down over Vietnam, but had somehow survived a long, tortuous capture by the Viet Cong. He was a great hero. A man all America admired.

Through his binoculars, Hack could clearly see the four attackers, each wearing a balaclava to protect their identity. They were scrambling to reload the RPG launcher. By their actions, Hack knew immediately they were experienced with weapons. No time to give them another chance to prove it.

Just then, a single shot sounded above the White House.

The combatant, holding the long brown metal launcher on his right shoulder, fell to the ground, shot through the front of his head. Dead!

The weapon landed next to him, directly in front of the comrade still holding a green rocket grenade in his two rubber-gloved hands.

Panic and fear now shifted to the lawn of The Ellipse.

Another rifle shot. Down he went, falling backwards, the RPG-7 falling straight to the ground.

The other two looked up toward the White House.

"Run! Run!" yelled a twenty-something, long-haired and bearded leader. Before he could take his first step, a third shot rang out. Right through the heart. Down he went. Dead before he hit the ground.

The three were sprawled only a few feet apart across the grass of President's Park. Dead! Blood poured out like a stream of departing evil, filling the dirt patches in the thick green lawn.

The fourth attacker dropped his rifle and sprinted south as fast as he could possibly run, hoping to escape the range of Hack's rifle.

Running hard but looking over his shoulder, he couldn't find the black Suburban SUV that was supposed to pick up the assault team immediately after the attack. He was on his own. He huffed and puffed with each step, his eyes wide, his mouth open, sprinting with every ounce of energy he had in his unconditioned, unathletic body. Then, he could hear something hit the ground just behind him. A bullet, he thought. He kept running, sprinting. Then, a stinging sensation filled the back of his right thigh. It knocked him to the ground.

He struggled to get up.

Hack took another look through his binoculars. He watched the assailant pull the balaclava off his head and his long hair fall out. He was just a kid, thought Hack. A kid who was in great pain, trying to get up and escape.

Hack could have finished him off easily. But no. This young, bearded, brown-haired, pudgy-looking assailant would be kept alive for an interrogation, to find out who was behind this plot to attack the White House.

As the injured combatant rose to his feet, whoosh! A burning sensation filled his upper right thigh. Down he went. Both legs had been shot and were badly bleeding. He was going nowhere except lockup, where he would be questioned. And they would get answers.

A few seconds later, a half dozen police from the SWAT tactical unit arrived at the scene. Guns were drawn, locked and loaded. One false move, and the bleeding boy on the ground would be the dead boy on the ground. Within minutes, the tactical unit had him handcuffed and led to their armored SWAT vehicle twenty-five yards away.

Just then, two American fighter jets buzzed over the White House, the pilots looking for any enemy combatants on the ground or in the air.

Police and fire sirens blared down Pennsylvania and Constitution Avenues. It seemed all of D.C. was being showered with blue and red flashing lights, bouncing off the buildings along 16th Street.

Three Mohawk helicopters appeared in the distance, heading toward the White House, armed and ready to fire.

Hack looked up and smiled. The power of the U.S. military had shown up within minutes of the attack. It was reassuring, filling him with a great sense of confidence and pride. At the same time, he felt a strong sense of remorse, so angry that someone had been able to fire two RPGs into the Oval Office, which had been totally destroyed, leaving a gaping hole at the center of the White House.

Smoke was pouring out, creating a huge rising cloud of grey and black from the massive fire inside. Hack was praying President Fallon hadn't been in there when the missile had hit.

He scanned the park for any other combatants, anyone who looked even remotely concerned about the three dead men lying on the park's trampled grass. This was a protocol he had followed nearly every day that he had fought in Afghanistan, so he was quite adept at spotting the enemy.

The two fighter jets buzzed the White House again. That was when Hack heard on the Secret Service Radio that the President had been in the workout room when the RPG had hit. He was fine and had been immediately rushed down to the Emergency Operations Center under the East Wing of the White House.

A big smile grew from the Director's square jaw.

The attackers had damaged the Oval Office. So what? That could be fixed. The President was alive! That was all that mattered.

The Mohawks had arrived. One landed on the south lawn of the White House. The other moved slowly over The Ellipse, two soldiers scanning President's Park with their active illumination night vision goggles, looking for enemy combatants.

Hack knew the drill. Those birds could take off and strike any opposing force within seconds. He loved the Mohawks. He had had plenty of experience working in them, and with them, in Afghanistan.

At that moment, Hack watched a black SUV pull up in front of the three downed attackers. Another twenty-something man, with long black hair and a bulging backpack, ran around to the back of the vehicle and opened the back hatch. He then sprinted to the three fallen attackers.

The SWAT team still hadn't arrived. Hack watched the man grab one of the dead men and drag him toward the SUV, lifting him up and pushing him into the back.

"Where's that SWAT team?" Hack barked over the radio system, which now had the police and National Guard on the frequency. "They should have been there by now."

"Right here, Hack," blared out FBI SWAT team leader, Commander Dirk Williams, speeding toward The Ellipse. "We're nearly there!"

Hack was growing impatient. There was no way he was going to allow that kid to load up his three dead comrades and escape. He hoped SWAT could get there before he had to stop him.

The dark-haired kid was dressed in the same black garb the other four had been wearing, so he was most certainly part of the assault team. After loading the second dead man into the black Suburban, he started looking around to see if anyone had noticed him. Then, he stood and turned toward the White House. A look of great anger filled the binoculars. That was all Hack needed to see.

A moment later, as the kid ran over to pick up the third dead man, blam! The sound of another rifle shot rang out. The bullet pierced through the young man in black's upper left thigh, and he recoiled backwards and to the ground. Blam! A blast filled his right leg. Hack wasn't going to let this enemy assailant escape. But he wasn't going to kill him, either. Now they had two enemy combatants to answer questions.

Writhing in anguish and grabbing at his bleeding legs, the kid screamed out, "Lucas! Lucas! Where are you? Lucas!"

The crowd, which had fled away from the burning White House and into the park, seemed to turn in unison toward the screaming man. All could see the lone dead man on the ground with a black wool hat covering his face.

The long, pointed green grenade lying on the ground filled in the blanks. Most ran. A few remained. One young man in a Cleveland Indians baseball cap walked up to the scene. He stood looking at the dead man and the screaming man next to him.

"Help me, buddy!" said the screaming man. "Get me into my truck!"

The Indians fan ignored his plea. He bent down over one of the semi-automatic rifles on the ground.

"Don't do it, kid!" muttered Hack to himself as he watched him through his binoculars.

As he examined the AK-15, he could hear a whoosh, a loud clink against the gun, which spun ten feet away. The boy jolted straight up and looked around, raising his hands, hoping not to be shot.

"That's better," Hack thought. "Now walk away."

He did. The once-curious, but now terribly shaken, man kept his hands in the air and walked toward the stream of white SUV police vehicles with flashing blue lights and loud sirens imposing their will on the entire area. The man ran up to the first cop he could find and reported what had just happened to him.

At that moment, Commander Williams and his SWAT team screeched up to the scene in their impressive black armored vehicle, parking in front of the black SUV with the opened back hatch. At the same time, a green U.S. Army truck filled with a National Guard unit drove in from the west side. A dozen armed soldiers, fully dressed for battle, jumped off the truck.

The six-member SWAT team emptied out of the black armored vehicle. Semi-automatic rifles at the ready, they jogged quickly toward the dead man and the screaming man a few yards away.

Ambulance sirens were close.

Williams and his men checked the dead.

Two red-and-white-colored ambulances jumped the curb and parked on the grass. Two of the paramedics were directed toward the screaming young man with blood pouring out his leg.

"We made a huge mistake listening to that asshole!" moaned the badly injured man to the young beautiful brunette paramedic who was working quickly to clean and bandage his bleeding legs. "Those were my friends that got killed. They're dead, and I can't walk. I knew this wasn't going to work! Asshole!"

While the paramedics were working on the driver of what was supposed to be the getaway vehicle, the National Guard cordoned off the area. A tall, thin sergeant in riot gear, holding a megaphone in his right hand, instructed civilians to evacuate the area.

Following their training to the letter, the soldiers moved people out in an orderly fashion. They also looked for anyone who was noticeably angry, carrying a backpack or dressed in black—anyone or anything that looked suspicious.

A detailed description of the enemy attackers had been provided, so the soldiers knew exactly the type of person that could be a threat. Young, long hair, a beard, dressed in black.

As Hack watched the soldiers and SWAT team below, he was anxious to find out who was behind this attack on the White

House, President Fallon and the United States of America. He thought it had to be bigger than just a small group of young radicals. But who?

All Hack knew for certain was that the group or organization responsible for this attack would not get away with it. Not on his watch! He was an American through and through. He fought for his country. He would die for America. And he had faith that the FBI, Secret Service and the police would all work together to find the people behind this assault and bring them to justice.

CHAPTER TWO

The two battered and bruised men seated next to each other leaned on the old, worn rectangular wooden table. They could barely keep their painfully tired bloodshot eyes open. They were both exhausted, faces cut, bruised and bandaged.

The pudgy, bearded, shoulder-length-brown-haired, twenty-one-year-old man on the right had white linen bandages covering the semi-repaired gunshot wounds in his left and right thighs, from the quickie surgery performed by the brunette paramedic. He was sweating profusely, still in tremendous agony from the bullets Ken Hack had put into his legs as he had fled through President's Park an hour earlier.

Sitting next to him was the fifth man directly involved with the White House attack. Bent over, gasping in pain, his long black hair resting on the old pine table, bandages turning brown from the still-seeping thigh wounds. He continued moaning with great discomfort.

A moment later, the imposing 6'2" figure entered the interrogation room. Ken Hack sat down in the chair across from the two men and looked at them squirming, sweating, moaning.

"Okay, now, I can see you are quite uncomfortable," he began, taking a sip of the water on the table. "Well, I can end your torment in a matter of minutes. Just tell me who you are working for. Who hatched this attack on the White House?"

"We are with the Democratic Party," snarled Austin Lucas, the pudgy twenty-one-year-old, grimacing through the pain. "We take our orders from the Democratic leadership in Congress."

"That's funny!" smirked Hack. "I know the Democrats aren't

fond of President Fallon, but even they wouldn't go this far. So cut the clowning, dipshit. Who's behind this?"

The second man, twenty-five-year-old Michael Johns, whom Hack recognized as the angry face through his binoculars, answered, "We're behind this! That's who! There were only five of us, and we blew up the White House. We don't need this government telling us what to do! And now we have sent that message directly to the Oval Office. There's more of us, too. This isn't over!"

Hack paused, soaking in that diatribe of questionable information. "What's the name of your organization? Where are you from? Who's funding this?" Hack demanded.

Heavy breathing. Loud moaning bounced off the light green walls of the empty room. Hack watched, waiting for answers.

Johns looked up at him. "You want to know who we are? Is that what you want to know?"

"Yeah, that's what I want to know!"

"And you'll get us back into our hospital beds?"

"Right away!" responded Hack skeptically, wondering if any semblance of truth would be forthcoming.

"Okay," Johns began, "We are with an organization called… The Rockettes."

Hack stared at the comedian with total disgust.

"We are from New York City, and we are funded by the Macy's Day Parade. So there! Now get the nurses and get us back to our rooms."

Lucas couldn't hold back his laughter, but then the results of those comments became all too clear. "That's not true, Michael," Lucas interrupted. "Tell him the truth. We need more medical attention now!"

Hack turned toward Lucas, "And…"

"We are working for…"

Hack listened.

"We are working for a man named… Mouse. Yeah, a Mr. Mickey Mouse."

Now Johns began laughing. "That's goofy," he added.

"Oh, yeah. Him, too. Goofy is the brains of the operation."

Both terrorists began laughing at their own silly jokes, dismissing the fact that they could die if they weren't monitored and treated for infection fairly quickly.

Hack just shook his head. "You know, for two guys who really need an antibiotic injection pretty quickly here, before an infection sets in, I would think you would be a little smarter and cooperate with some legitimate answers."

Hack then stood up and leaned across the table, looking directly into the eyes of the two men in agony. "I'm sure you realize we have *all* of the information from your other three associates, as well as both of your backgrounds—where you are from, where you live, where your families live," he informed them, communicating a direct threat to their families. "We know you are members of the violent leftist group called 1917. And the FBI knows exactly where to find them. And we will!"

"You can't scare us!" Johns snapped at him. "Now we want our lawyers."

Laughter could be heard from outside the makeshift interrogation room.

Hack looked back, giving the two FBI agents peering in the door behind him a nasty look.

Laughter ceased. Hack looked back at the two comedians, who seemed to have lost their sense of humor for the moment. "You have no rights here," he informed them. "You're terrorists. Domestic terrorists! The worst kind! Why did you attack the White House?"

Silence. Hack watched them squirm.

Lucas looked uneasy. "It wasn't my idea!" blurted out Lucas, now ready to talk.

"Shut up, Lucas!" scolded his associate.

"No, Michael! I need medical attention now!"

The men sat silent, while continuing to writhe in pain, breathing heavily, sweat dripping onto the table.

"Okay, well, your fever will increase over the next hour." Hack informed them about their near future. "The infection will take hold, and chances are, you'll both be dead by noon tomorrow—two o'clock at the latest. And take a look around the room. This is where you will stay until the coroner's office comes to haul away your bodies."

"He's right!" Lucas appealed. "I'll talk!"

"You do, and you're a dead man!" Johns shouted.

"I'm going to die if I don't get help!"

"They have to give us medical attention. They have to give us a lawyer, despite what this asshole is telling us."

Lucas fell silent and looked up at Hack.

Realizing the interrogation was over for the moment, the White House's top Secret Service agent stood straight up, turned and walked toward the door. Then, he stopped and looked over his shoulder at the two men in misery. "Now, if you change your minds and would like to be more cooperative, just let us know. I'm the guy who shot you in the legs so you would have a chance to live another day… I could have killed you both. So you're on borrowed time as it is right now."

"You're the one who shot us?" yelled out Johns. "You bastard! We'll get you! I can promise you that. We may die here tonight, but our boys will get you!"

Hack smiled sarcastically, listening to a man with no cards left on the table trying to threaten him. "Well, you be sure to tell your boys, Mickey and Goofy, that they can find me at the real Hall of Presidents," informed Hack, now the one making the bad jokes. "And they'd better come locked and loaded."

He exited the medical office and spoke with the two FBI agents outside the door.

"Get the nurses, and get these two back to their rooms," Hack directed. "I'll get them a lawyer."

"You're so close," said one of the agents, a bit frustrated by Hack's willingness to help so quickly.

"They will die if we don't get them help now," implored Hack, looking through the glass at them one more time. "Hell, it's probably fifty-fifty at best now, anyway. But get them help. Immediately!"

At that moment, Hack's phone buzzed as a text came in. He glanced at it. "I've got to go to FBI headquarters," he told the two agents guarding the terrorists. "You've got my number, if you need me right away."

CHAPTER THREE

News of the attack on the White House shook America.

On every news channel, coverage showed the burning Oval Office, with grey smoke continuing to smolder out of the massive, gaping hole.

Each outlet repeatedly showed this visual. As with 9/11, most Americans were devastated by the coverage but continued to watch in total disbelief, creating a traumatized nation from coast to coast.

Unlike 9/11, this attack on America had not been conducted by al-Qaeda. It had been perpetrated by a group of young white kids. Young men. Angry, rebellious Americans!

Who were they? And why had they attacked the White House? And where had they gotten the weapons and training to execute such a plan?

Analysts on USA News immediately positioned the attacks as political vengeance from the far-left wing in the country, the Democratic socialists who hated President Fallon. Conducting the attack on May 1, International Workers Day, supported the speculation that it had been an attack by radical, communist leftists in America.

The other two major cable networks, LNN and CBN, reported the attack in a more defensive manner. From the anchor desk throughout the day, it was reported as just another domestic attack in a continuing series of attacks that had occurred in the United States over the past two decades. Nothing new! Nothing to be overly concerned about!

This debate between news organizations created a much-needed education for Americans about the domestic attacks that had taken place in the country. Chet Phare, the highly regarded anchor at USA

News, presented a one-hour special report to provide a historical perspective.

"The deadliest and most well-known homegrown attack in the history of the United States was the Oklahoma City Bombing on April 19, 1995," Phare reported, showing the disturbing images of the blown-out government building and badly injured victims being tended to by paramedics. "This massive damage was brought about by two vengeful Americans, Terry Nichols and Timothy McVeigh, both former U.S. Army soldiers who had fought together in the Gulf War."

Photographs of McVeigh in his army uniform appeared. He looked like the clean-cut American boy next door. Not quite!

As members of a survivalist group, McVeigh and Nichols had wanted revenge against the government, and specifically the FBI, U.S. Marshall Police and the Bureau of Alcohol, Tobacco and Firearms Police. The coordinated effort of those government agencies, in August of 1992, seeking to apprehend Randy Weaver at his cabin on Ruby Ridge near Naples, Idaho, had resulted in a six-team U.S. Marshall shooting Weaver's son Sammy and their dog. Then, an FBI sniper, Lon Horiuchi, had shot and killed Weaver's wife, Vicki, as she stood in the doorway, trying to get her wounded husband into the cabin. This was followed by the same government enforcement groups' botched three-month takeover of the Branch Davidian's compound in Waco, Texas beginning on February 28, 1993.

"For two years, anger festered in the minds of McVeigh and Nichols, who hatched a revengeful plan to get back at the government," Phare continued, with video of the burning Waco compound on the screen. "In April of 1995, Nichols helped pack a Ryder rental truck with five thousand pounds of explosives, which McVeigh parked in front of the Alfred P. Murrah Federal Building on the morning of April 19. The massive explosion occurred at 9:02 that morning, blowing half of the building apart and killing one hundred and sixty-eight innocent people, including nineteen children. More than six hundred and eighty others were injured, and thirty-five other buildings in the area were severely damaged."

Dylan Reilly sat in his West Loop condo in Chicago, watching this coverage. As a history teacher, he was quite familiar with most of the domestic attacks being reported by Phare. He certainly knew the details of the Oklahoma City bombing, Eric Rudolph's Centennial Olympic Park bombing, and Ted Kaczynski's seventeen-year letter-bomb campaign against academics and tech experts.

The report on the bomb set off on September 15, 1963 by the United Klans of America at the 16th Street Baptist Church in Birmingham, Alabama was a historical event he had taught each year at Watson College Prep. He was always more than a bit surprised that most of the students weren't familiar with that horrific explosion that had killed four young black girls.

Watching this retrospective, Dylan was glad the country was being reminded that America, like all countries, was filled with citizens with different points of view, different perspectives. While most would engage in an argument or debate over issues, sometimes those differences could result in tragic violence, set off by a seemingly simple act.

That point came to light during Phare's report on the 1921 Tulsa Race Massacre, which really got Reilly's attention, because he had never heard of it. Phare showed old, grainy black-and-white photos of the major race riot that erupted in Tulsa, Oklahoma on May 31, 1921.

"It all started when Dick Rowland, a nineteen-year-old black shoeshine boy, got onto an elevator as he was returning from the washroom on the top floor of the Drexel office building," Phare explained. "A scream on the elevator, followed by a witness claiming to see Rowland running out of the elevator doors, resulted in a claim of attempted rape by Sarah Page, a seventeen-year-old white elevator operator.

"Rowland was arrested that day, and the story remains unclear, but historians speculate that the scream was a result of Rowland accidently stepping on Page's foot."

A photo of Rowland appeared on the screen.

"Up until that point, it could have been a misunderstanding that would be resolved in the courtroom. But the *Tulsa Tribune* reported that Rowland would be lynched for his alleged crime, which hadn't even been tried at that point," reported Phare, who went on to describe how that news report had resulted in large crowds of black and white citizens lining up outside the courthouse. Among the crowd was a group of black World War I veterans who twice offered the Tulsa Police assistance to protect Rowland. As they were leaving, a white man grabbed one of their guns, and a shot was fired.

And that one act, a man grabbing for the gun, set off total bedlam. White and black citizens began battling on the ground throughout Tulsa's all-black Greenwood district, while in the air, six two-seat, single engine Curtis airplanes were used to drop some form of firebombs onto the roofs of black homes and businesses. This was the first aerial attack on the United States in the country's history.

When the dust had settled, the death toll, like the start of the riot, was unclear. Historians said it was most likely somewhere between twenty-four and thirty-eight, where others reported that it was as high as three hundred. One thing was clear. More than 1,500 black homes had been burned to the ground and 600 black-owned businesses bombed. Of the district's black population of 10,000, nearly 6,000 had been placed by the National Guard in the Convention Hall and the Fairgrounds facilities for eight days.

Watching this report with great interest and dismay, since he had never read about this historical event before, Dylan stood from his couch and walked over to his five-row oak bookshelf. From the top shelf, he grabbed the two American history books from which he taught at the high school. Checking the index of both, he found no listing for the Tulsa Massacre. He shook his head and made a mental note of it, hoping to bring it up at some point. He was just glad Chet Phare had covered it. He was sure millions, like him, had learned something new and important about America's history.

Absorbing everything that he had just watched after the devastating attack on the White House, Dylan felt a strong responsibility to help the authorities find the people responsible and bring them to justice. He suspected the assault was not the sole responsibility of a small group of angry young men, as was being widely reported. It had to go far deeper, far higher.

He pulled out his red-white-and-blue-covered cell phone and called his friend, Captain Gregory Panozzo at Chicago Police Headquarters.

"Hey, Greg. It's Dylan," announced Reilly, a smile growing on his face, hearing his good friend's strong Chicago accent loud and clear through his new iPhone 6s. "You got time to meet? I want to see if I can get involved in this investigation into the White House attack."

They scheduled a meeting at Chicago Police Headquarters, at 3510 South Michigan Avenue, just a hop, skip and a jump from three of the offices that famed mobster Al Capone had used during his bootlegging days in the 1920s. Dylan loved passing by those historical landmarks and pointing them out to friends, most of whom were completely uninterested.

As he entered the revolving glass door, a tall African American police officer at the security checkpoint blurted out, "Hello, Mr. Reilly, nice to see you again!" Dylan shook hands with him and began taking out his keys and phone to place them in a small gray basket that would be run through the scanner.

"No need for that," said the smiling officer, guiding the famed hero through the walk-through metal detector, which lit up and beeped loudly as he passed through with plenty of metal on him, including his famous six-shooter. This got the attention of everyone in the lobby. Within seconds, Dylan was greeted by a surge of young and old police officers and administrative personnel. They were all grateful for Dylan's efforts the year before and quite thrilled to see him walk in the door once again.

Smiles beamed around the large lobby with a circular silver desk at the center. There were handshakes, hugs and of course, several requests to see the famed silver Smith and Wesson six-shooter.

Cell phones were out and ready for photos, keepsakes each would most certainly share with family and friends, to be sure.

Out the corridor to Dylan's right emerged the familiar 5'9", dark-haired and muscular Captain Panozzo, who had been promoted after his heroic acts at the Midwest Trade Building. He was ecstatic to see his old friend.

"Hey, Greg!" Dylan smiled. "How's my favorite cop?"

"Oh, I'm good, DR," replied the smiling middle-aged Italian American, who had grown up in Riverside, a suburb just west of Chicago. "I'm hoping we can figure out something here today. It would be good to get you involved. C'mon back to my office, and we can talk about it."

In the short time since Dylan's arrival, the small group of men and women in blue grew to about thirty. A sea of iPhones was held high, as people tried to get a photo of their famed associate as he led "The Fastest Gun" through the main corridor.

Dylan noticed that one of the staffers wasn't taking photos and had a stern look on his face as he watched the welcome party. He made a mental note of the Middle Eastern-looking man with the dark skin, in his early thirties, fairly short and thin, with long black hair, dressed in a wrinkled white dress shirt and rumpled khaki pants.

As he exited with Captain Greg down the main hallway, Dylan took a glance back at the man with angry eyes. "Greg, who's that guy back there, with the dark hair and khaki pants?"

"Oh, I'm sure that's just one of the interns, working in the administrative offices here," he said, taking a good look at the man, who noticed the attention he was receiving and quickly darted out of the lobby.

"Okay," agreed Dylan. "Something's not right there. Keep your eye on him. It may be nothing, but…"

"Oh, yeah. Don't worry. I'll have someone watch him," the captain responded, never underestimating Dylan's instincts.

Halfway down the corridor, Dylan could see straight out the glass doors and into the parking lot. There stood the famous bronze statue of a policeman that had been unveiled in the middle of Haymarket Square on May 30, 1889 to honor Mathias Degan, one of the seven police officers killed in the line of duty during the riot that had taken place there.

The statue, designed by Frank Batchelder, presented the police officer with his right arm raised and the inscription on the pedestal below reading, "In the name of the People of Illinois, I command peace." The much-traveled and famed statue now sat just outside police headquarters, in a fenced-off parking lot where no one could destroy it. As a history buff and teacher, Dylan loved seeing the statue, well aware of the incredible history behind it, which he thought he would share with his pal Greg.

"Can we take another peek at the statue, Greg?" asked Dylan.

"Of course," he confirmed, taking Dylan through the glass doors and into the parking lot. "This seems to be the only place in the city where we know we can protect it."

Dylan marveled at the bronze policeman and the impressive detail of the figure initially created by sculptor Johannes Gelert. The nine-foot-tall monument had been damaged, repaired and moved several times. That fact, in and of itself, was evidence of the ongoing and longstanding battle between the police and groups of socialists and anarchists.

That battle had begun on May 4, 1927, when the driver of a streetcar steered the vehicle into the police memorial because he was tired of seeing the policeman with his arm raised. The city had restored the statue and a year later, placed it in Union Park, which was not the best choice, given the history of the park. However, thirty years later, it was moved back to its original location in Haymarket Square, overlooking a brand-new expressway. That didn't last.

During the summer of 1968, the 82nd anniversary of the statue, a group of Vietnam protestors wishing to show their total disrespect for the police, sprayed black paint across it. They returned a year later on October 6 and placed a bomb between the policeman's legs, blowing the statue to smithereens.

The then-infamous anarchist group, the Weatherman, claimed responsibility.

After legendary Chicago Mayor Richard J. Daley had the statue restored, he unveiled it on May 4, 1970. However, the Weatherman returned to blow it up again on October 6 of that year.

Daley, known as the last big city "Boss" in America, was not one to let radicals defeat him. He had the statue repaired one more time and placed a twenty-four-hour police guard at the memorial. In 1972, given the annual cost of the guard, Daley had the statue moved to Chicago Police Headquarters, located at 1100 South State, where it would be safe.

Then, in October of 1976, during the final few months of his life, Daley moved the statue one more time, placing it in the enclosed courtyard of the Chicago Police Academy. That seemed to make sense.

But in 2007, his son, Richard M. Daley, was the mayor and had the statue moved to the new police headquarters on South Michigan Avenue, with a new pedestal, unveiled by Geraldine Doceka, Officer Mathias Degan's great-granddaughter.

The original pedestal had been left in Haymarket Square, where it became an anarchist landmark, covered with graffiti until it was taken down in 1986.

Unlike the Tulsa Race Massacre, the Haymarket Riot was included in history books. The violence and chaos that took place in Chicago was the result of mostly German workers striking to get an eight-hour workday, while company owners brought in strikebreakers to take their place, with Pinkerton guards to protect them.

Socialist and anarchist groups latched onto the widespread and growing anger among the working men. They saw an opportunity to turn America toward socialism.

On May 1, workers at the McCormick Harvester Works plant called for a general strike. More than 400 police were called in to guard the strikebreakers as they entered the plant. Two days later, striking workers attacked the scabs as they exited the plant, and police opened fire, killing two of the workers.

A revenge rally was immediately organized to take place on May 4 in Haymarket Square, a very busy business center at the time. The thousands of flyers distributed read, *"Revenge! Workingmen to Arms!"* More than 2,000 protestors showed up while police watched from wagons parked off to the side of Randolph Street.

Initially, the rally was calm. Even Mayor Carter Harrison Sr. attended to watch but left when it looked like everything was in order except for the poor weather. But at 10:30 that night, just as Methodist pastor, socialist and anarchist, Samuel Fielden, was finishing his speech atop a wagon, the police lined up in a formation of three rows and moved toward the wagon and protestors to end the rally and clear the streets.

That was when a dynamite bomb filled with metal casings was ignited by a fuse and thrown at the front of the advancing police line. The explosion and flying metal fragments killed seven of the cops and wounded six others.

Like Tulsa, all hell broke loose, with gunfire exchanged from both sides. The police shot at the fleeing demonstrators, killing four and wounding approximately seventy more. Besides the seven dead police officers, sixty others had been wounded.

Within five minutes, Haymarket Square was empty, except for the dead and wounded lying on the cold, wet orange-bricked street. Germans and Bohemians, who made up the majority of the protestors, were being blamed for the riot.

"It's not so different than what we are dealing with today, don't you think, Greg?" asked Dylan, taking out his iPhone to take a photo of the legendary statue. "I mean, certainly the circumstances are different. Back then, owners were overworking and underpaying their workforce, and when the workers revolted, anarchists saw an opportunity and capitalized on it. Now, people are upset about the police officer shooting the teenager. The media plays up the controversy and protests begin. And once again, anarchists and socialists are trying to capitalize on it."

"I think you're right, DR," his friend nodded. "They know they can't just go out and call for Americans to turn the country into a socialist state. They have to weave themselves into already established anger, rampant unrest, and try to guide it toward their political views. That's what they've done for quite a long time now, in this country. You'd think people would catch on."

The two friends then walked back inside to Captain Panozzo's corner office to plan how Dylan could use his talents to help stop the attacks.

CHAPTER FOUR

It was an exciting time for the four students from College of Illinois University (CIU). They each had been personally recruited into an organization that promised to change the world. Individually, each had hopes of making a difference, a positive impact, a better country for all.

Although the four young men had never met before, each seemed to recognize the others sitting around the large, old oak table centered in the dining room of the greystone home in Wrigleyville, on Chicago's North Side.

On this rainy Sunday morning, their lack of preparation was apparent on their soaked shirts. It was a strange scene to enter for their first official meeting. Around the table sat anxious expectation and disorganization. Sunday newspapers were scattered across the floor. Empty beer and whiskey bottles filled the kitchen counter to the side.

Perhaps it had just been a college party the night before. Possibly a great celebration had taken place. Maybe they would be part of the next one. Regardless, they were ready for their orientation.

Jeffrey Wooten, a tall, thin, brown-bearded, balding man in his early thirties, sat in the high-backed brown oak chair at the head of the table. It was apparent that he was no student. He was the oldest in the group and the leader.

Wooten was a strange character. He had grown up on a dairy farm in upstate New York, before moving to Evanston, where his accent had created problems for him among the North Shore's tough guys.

The Murphy brothers, known as the bully boys in the neighborhood, used Wooten as their punching bag, just for fun, on many a Friday evening. Four years of being bullied had made Wooten an angry young man, which only increased as he entered his twenties, bouncing from job to job, and his irritated demeanor was usually at fault for the pink slip or escort out the door.

To his left sat his best friend, Raul Fontane, a short, dark-haired, heavy-set computer tech, also in his early thirties. He had grown up in a small, three-bedroom, red brick home in Evanston, across the street from Wooten.

Raul was generally considered a nerd by his classmates, a social pariah who literally had no friends, until his path crossed with Wooten's one Friday night at the township's high school football game.

On Raul's trip to the men's room, Andy Murphy, the oldest of the thug brothers, had stepped in his way and told him he needed to pay the washroom toll of $5 or he couldn't let him pass. Fontane turned to walk away and felt a sharp pain across the back of his head.

When he awoke, he was lying face down on the cinder-covered path. As he rose to his feet, he saw his neighbor, Wooten, lying twenty-five feet away, bloodied and beaten. A close bond was formed that evening.

From that night forward, Fontane and Wooten had been lifelong friends who had committed allegiance to each other, "no matter what comes our way!" That was their promise to each other, and they both fully intended to commit to it.

Next to Fontane at the table sat Rob Slagle, a twenty-something, out-of-shape, long dark-haired hipster with a half-grown goatee. Slagle was from Manhattan, New York and had come to Chicago upon the recommendation of a fellow he had met in his apartment building on 11th Avenue. He had hopes of becoming a comedian and was told CIU had excellent improv teachers who came from the famed Second Tier Theater Company.

Like Wooten and Fontane, Slagle too had been a social outcast during his high school years in New York, where he had unsuccessfully attempted to inject his very strange and perverse sense of humor into social situations to gain friends. So despite his hopes of becoming a famous comedian, the moment he was approached at CIU and offered the opportunity to join the group, he didn't have to be asked twice.

On the other side of the table sat Darius Ramirez, a smart, physically fit sophomore at CIU, of average height and with distinctive jet-black hair combed to the side. He looked like an athlete and a dead ringer for the actor, Mario Lopez. He had been in so many fights at Payne Tech High School, and sent to the principal's office so often, that he had lost all regard for authority. When approached to join the group and stand up to the country's biggest authoritarian, the government, he couldn't say yes fast enough.

Next to him sat Tim Kamus a tall, prematurely balding brown-haired sophomore at CIU with an average build and noticeable bow-legged walk. Kamus was a marketing major with plans to go into the medical field. Having been raised in a wealthy family in Northbrook, he wanted to help the common man, the little guy.

At the other end of the table sat Ron Clapp, a bulging-eyed, balding twenty-three-year-old senior at CIU who was working in the customer service department at Sears in Schaumburg, where Wooten had met him and recruited him into the group. Clapp always boasted about being a lifelong Democrat, a far-left extremist who hated all Republicans, all conservatives, and would do anything he could defeat them. Wooten's offer to join the group was completely in line with Clapp's politics and mindset.

A knock at the door.

"Raul, get the door," directed Wooten, somewhat anxious about this meeting. A few seconds later, his best friend returned with a grey-haired, middle-aged man of average height, wearing a custom-tailored Kiton grey suit.

All eyes around the table stared at the visitor with the hard, leather-skinned and wrinkled face. His beady eyes, big chin, big ears, prominent nose and full lips, gave him the appearance of a very serious and dangerous man. This was not the type of person the four students at the table were accustomed to seeing on the CIU campus.

"Mr. Medov, thank you for you coming," welcomed Wooten, rising from his chair to shake hands with the visitor. "As you can see, I've got my team assembled here, just as you requested. And we're ready to go!"

"Yes, I see that, Jeffrey," nodded the large, intimidating-looking man with a distinct Russian accent as he took a good look at the rag-tag group of men. Analyzing each of the faces around the table, he began taking off his gloves, pulling one finger at a time. Why he was wearing gloves in May was a mystery in and of itself. He set the black leather gloves on the counter next to the empty bottles and cans, then turned and looked directly at the curious young men.

"I want all of you here to know that this is not a one-time adventure," Medov announced in no uncertain terms. "Once you have joined this cause, it's a lifetime commitment. Do you understand?"

Silence.

One by one, Wooten read the reactions, the eyes of his five recruits. He had failed to mention that one minor detail when he had recruited them.

Medov paced the floor in front of the table.

This was most certainly unwelcome news to most of them, who thought they were just helping to organize a few demonstrations, protests against the cops and city government. They all hated the government, status quo, anyone in any position of authority. They had signed up to fight against it.

"Do you understand?" Medov demanded loudly.

The five inductees to the socialist cause half-heartedly nodded in agreement.

"What Mr. Medov is saying is that once you become a full-fledged socialist in this country, you will have that tag on you for life," explained Wooten, dressed in faded black jeans and a grey t-shirt that read, "RESIST!" in large red letters across the front.

"That's right, Jeffrey," Medov concurred. "The FBI won't remove that affiliation from your record, but neither will I. We can't afford deserters. It's too risky for the rest of us. Do you understand?"

Silence once again.

The bulging-eyed Clapp stood. "Look, I didn't really know the full extent of my commitment to the group," he admitted in a high-pitched nasally voice. "When Jeffrey asked me to join, you never said…"

"Well, you're in now, Ron! And there's no backing out!" Wooten stated in a low, threatening manner that got the attention, as well, of the other four, each of whom wanted to run out the door at that moment.

Medov put his hands behind his back and walked to the head of the table, standing next to Wooten, who offered him his chair. He declined and remained standing, while staring into the eyes of each unnerved comrade at the table, trying to ascertain if they really had the commitment to continue with the plan.

"Can I get you a drink?" asked Clapp, still standing, hoping to show his support.

Medov glanced at him but did not respond. Clapp sheepishly sat back down.

"This is the beginning of what needs to be a very effective assault on the government here in Chicago," expressed the Russian in a low tone. "You all need to understand. You are now part of something much bigger. This is going to happen here and in Washington, D.C. We need committed soldiers to achieve total success for our socialist mission to overthrow America. Do you understand?"

Silence. Curious looks. Fearful eyes. A glance at the door weighing the chances of running out before being caught.

Medov paused, continuing to analyze the true attitudes behind their faces. "So that's my question to each of you. Are you committed to the cause?"

Silence. Another glance toward the hallway. The door was only fifteen feet away.

"Yes, absolutely," committed Wooten, breaking the silence with a strong vocal conviction, intensely looking at each of his new recruits at the table. "Everyone is committed, right, comrades?"

"Definitely!" proclaimed Clapp, raising his hand like a teacher's pet. The others followed, like first-time skydivers, jumping into an unknown situation and possibly death.

"One hundred percent!"

"Yes!"

"Absolutely!"

Silence.

All eyes shifted to the corner of the table where Raul Fontane sat silently.

"Raul!" barked Wooten, not wishing to see his best friend get into serious trouble.

Fontane looked up. He scanned the faces of the other men in the room, looking for a supportive look. "Jeffrey, you never said..."

"Raul!" scolded Wooten.

Silence.

"Hey, I'm a computer guy," he informed them, pleading his case. "I got into this purely because Jeffrey is my best friend, and I thought I could help with logistics. That's all. I am just here to help. Logistics, you know?"

Silence filled the room again as all eyes remained on the now-sweating computer geek. He forced a smile, panning across the faces of his new socialist comrades at the table.

"Raul, we talked about this. I told you what you—what we—were getting into here," Jeffrey insisted now visibly frustrated. "You said you were in it with me every step of the way... every step of the way, Raul! Just say you're in. You're committed. That's all!"

"I know!" admitted Raul, jumping to his feet, frustrated at his own stupidity. "When it's an idea, it's one thing. But now that it's actually happening, that's an entirely different thing."

Wooten looked at Medov, then back at his friend, who continued to plead his case.

"I'm just being honest here, Jeffrey, I don't think I can continue. I don't think I can commit the way Mr. Medov wants me—wants us—to."

As he was saying the words, he could see the looks around the table grow highly concerned, afraid for him. That's when he realized the dangerous predicament he had now placed himself in.

Silence.

"But no one here has to worry about me after today, okay? No one!" Raul confidently assured them, nodding directly at Medov, hoping to receive a positive response or look. "I'll walk away from this and never speak a word of it to anyone. So you don't have to worry, okay? Jeffrey knows me better than anyone. There's no risk."

"Raul, just say you're in, and we can move on! Just say it!" Wooten pleaded.

Fontane was visibly shaking. He had been having second thoughts about joining his best friend's group from the moment he had agreed. For weeks, Fontane had felt so anxious and depressed that he had seriously considered committing suicide. That morning, before leaving for the meeting, he had stood looking into his mirror for ten minutes, repeating to himself, "You're a coward! A weasel! You're a worthless lowlife! A total coward!"

Unfortunately, for those who knew him well, especially Wooten, those words were one hundred percent true. He was too insecure, too weak, too stupid, and too manipulated to fully appreciate what he had signed up for until the moment it had actually occurred.

"Look, I joined this group hoping we could make things better in America," he pleaded, emphasizing his point with raised hands and a frozen smile. "I never realized that we were going to be trying to actually bring down the government and destroy America."

"Are you kidding me?" asked Wooten, now incredibly disappointed in his friend, especially stating this for the first time in front of Medov. "Raul, what's our group's slogan?"

"'Bring Down America!' Yes, I know. But I thought it meant the current state of America, not the entire country. Not really!"

"No, it means the entire country, dumbass!" Wooten screamed at the top of his lungs, having lost all patience with the one person on earth he had expected to support him regardless of the risks. "Did that not dawn on you when you heard our plans for the demonstrations?"

Seeing the disappointment and anger in Wooten's eyes, Fontane stood and began walking toward the door. "I'm sorry, Jeffrey," he cried, his shoulders slumped, head down. He couldn't look at the others around the table as he walked past them.

Wooten knew what this meant for his comrade, his best friend. He looked at Medov, whose face grew hard and angry as he watched dejection walk past him and toward the door. With each step, it felt like every nerve in Raul's body was screaming out. His heart pounding, sweat pouring down his face, his eyes blurry, buzzing in his head, he kept walking, hoping he would make it to the door.

"No, don't even think about it, Dmitri!" warned Wooten, grabbing the Russian's arm. "He's my friend! I'll take the blame!"

With great force, Medov yanked back his arm, knocking Wooten to the grey tiled floor. Then, Wooten watched the Russian reach into his suit coat, pulling out a shiny black Glock gun.

Eyes grew fearful around the table. Some looked for another exit to escape.

Medov began walking toward the door. Wooten jumped back up to his feet.

"C'mon, Dmitri, this isn't necessary," Wooten begged, darting over to the large angry man, once again grabbing his arm, trying to stop him.

The Russian quickly turned and pointed the gun at him. Wooten froze, threw his arms up in the air and backed up several steps.

"Sit down!" ordered Medov.

Wooten sat, but yelled, "Run, Raul, run!"

Fontane turned around as he heard his friend. He saw the Russian stepping into the hallway, holding a gun. Fear sent a bolt of electricity through his entire body. He ran the final ten feet to the door, grabbed the brass knob, and tried to open it as fast as he could.

Too late!

Blam! Blam!

Two shots through the back of his head. Blood splattered onto the brown-stained oak door and white wall next to it. Fontane dropped straight down onto the floor, his eyes wide open as blood poured from the wounds beneath his dark hair.

Wooten ran into the hall, staring in horror at his best friend. Dead! He kneeled down and took his only friend into his arms, crying uncontrollably. "Why? Why? Why?" he moaned, the Russian watching him. Medov looked at his gun, considering shooting Wooten as well, to avoid any thoughts of revenge. No, he would let Wooten live. He needed him, so he would take his chances.

Shock filled the faces of the other four young men at the table. If there had been any thoughts in their collective minds about leaving the organization, they ended at that moment. Now it was life or death with every decision they made, every word they uttered. The stakes were that high. The chain of command was that clear.

The Russians were calling the shots. If the five new socialists didn't go along, follow orders, succeed in their assignments, they too would receive two bullets in the back of the head.

Wooten felt numb, looking at his friend. Tears poured down his face. He was completely overwhelmed. Fontane was the only person on earth he loved, and now he was gone.

Wooten had talked Fontane into joining the socialist group, thinking they could make an impact and change the world. After this bloody Sunday morning, the tall, balding man knew the only thing that he would be changing was his attitude toward the mission. He would either have to become a cold-blooded, heartless killer like Medov or somehow find a way to disappear.

The same thoughts were running through the collective minds of his four remaining comrades, standing behind him, waiting for the moment they could leave the greystone in Wrigleyville—alive!

CHAPTER FIVE

After leaving Chicago Police Headquarters, Dylan Reilly felt compelled to visit St. Peter's Church in downtown Chicago.

This was the same church where he had heard the Just Defense homily a year earlier, which had emboldened him to keep fighting, keep defending against men of ill will. After that day in 2014, he had fallen in love with the beautiful sanctuary and always felt inspired attending mass or just stopping in for a prayer. That had been his intent on this day. Once again, he asked for God's guidance as he was about to enter into another dangerous situation.

Earlier that afternoon, Captain Panozzo had called the FBI in Washington, D.C. while Dylan sat in his office listening to the conversation. Upon hearing the request, the administrator answering the phone immediately patched the captain through to FBI Director, Sheldon Phillips.

Panozzo had no personal contacts at the FBI in Washington. But given the fact that he was offering the FBI a chance to have Dylan Reilly join the effort, who could say no to that?

"We don't need the help of Dylan Reilly or anyone from Chicago!" the loud voice of Director Phillips blared through the phone. "But thanks for your offer, Officer…"

"Panozzo."

"Panozzo! Now I've got work to do, so if you don't mind," finished Phillips, slamming the phone hard, the sound ringing into the ear of the helpful Chicago policeman, who quickly pulled his head back from the receiver. Dylan watched his now wide-eyed friend hang up the phone.

"What was that?" Dylan asked with great surprise.

"Well, apparently, the FBI Director is not a huge fan of Chicago or you," Panozzo opined, shaking his head in dismay. "No worries. There are other avenues."

Panozzo knew the FBI was protective about investigations but was certain they would be more than eager to have Dylan join the effort to track down the people who had orchestrated the attack. He was wrong. Lesson learned. He called his Chicago FBI contact.

An hour later, Dylan was kneeling in the fifth row from the altar on the right side of the center aisle. He prayed five Our Fathers and five Hail Mary's, then asked for help,

"God, please show me the way on this new journey to defend innocent people against the ill will of those who wish to hurt them, kill them, tear down our country, our way of life, our peaceful society," he prayed with his head bowed against his praying hands. "If it is Your will to have me help, I will do everything I can, using the talents You gave me. I know You will guide me. I know You will show me the way. Jesus, I trust in You!"

He made the sign of the cross and sat back in the pew, gazing at the bright white crucifix centered at the back of the altar, a white statue of Mary looking up on the right and the distraught apostle John, head bowed, on the left. This recreation of Christ's crucifixion was set against an orange background to highlight the reverent scene.

Just then, Father Patrick Quilty, a Franciscan priest dressed in the order's brown cassock, approached him.

"Hello, Dylan," greeted the jovial priest, whom Dylan had come to know quite well since his visit to the confessional more than a year earlier.

"Hello, Father Pat," smiled Dylan, happy to see the priest whom he knew he could trust with his life. "How are you?"

"Well, better, much better, since you came into our lives," laughed the smiling Irish priest, as he sat down in the pew next to Dylan. "Do you know that more than fifteen hundred people have registered as parishioners here since it became known that you attend our church?"

"Really?" Dylan asked, more than a little surprised. "Fifteen hundred?"

"Fifteen hundred! And they are continuing to come in each week. Haven't you noticed how packed the church is during mass each Sunday?"

"I did notice that, yes, but I wasn't sure why…"

"You are why!" commented the fairly fit, grey-haired, affable priest. "People want to be in the church where a man of such conviction goes to practice his faith. But they also want to see you. Haven't you been approached by any of them?"

"Yes, more than a few. And it's a bit awkward, giving autographs here in God's house," he admitted, glancing around the church and noticing several people staring at him. "I'm a bit uncomfortable with all of it. But I am glad they're here. That's encouraging!"

"It is, yes," agreed Father Quilty, a lifelong Chicagoan who had grown up on the southwest side of the city. "So our pastor, whom you now know well, Father Carl Naso, was hoping you may be interested in getting a little more involved."

"More involved?"

"Yes. Would you be interested in being a reader?"

"Oh, I see. Well, I have been a reader at my other parishes."

"We think parishioners seeing you up on the altar, reading from the Bible, will provide even greater encouragement, inspiration. We think it would be very helpful!"

"Can I think about it?" Dylan asked, not wishing to offend the priest whom he admired for his integrity and loyalty.

"Certainly," offered the middle-aged priest, who had been inspired to enter the seminary in his thirties, giving up on a promising sales career in the electronics manufacturing industry in Minneapolis. "Even if you can only participate every now and then, we would appreciate it. People will be so excited to see you up there, Dylan. They really will! I will, too!"

"Thanks, Father Pat. Just give me a few days, and I'll get back to you about it, okay?"

"Sounds good. We will look forward to it," proclaimed the priest, who then stood and walked toward the back of the church. As Dylan watched him leave, he noticed that the dark-skinned Middle Eastern man, the angry intern from police headquarters, was sitting in the back pew.

Surprised, Dylan immediately stood and began walking down the center aisle, toward the back of the church. The short, thin, thirty-something rose quickly and walked out the glass doors of the sanctuary. As Dylan drew closer, he could see him run down the steps and out the large golden doors onto Madison Street.

He followed him, but by the time he reached the street, he was gone. No worries, he thought, then texted a note to Captain Panozzo.

I'm at St. Peter's and that intern we saw today was sitting in the back row. He obviously followed me. Please check him out. Something's up.

Standing on Madison, Dylan scanned the area for any sign of the man stalking him.

Father Patrick came out the door and down the steps, a bit winded.

"Everything okay, Dylan?" asked the priest, breathing heavily.

"Yes, Father Pat. That kid that just flew out the front door…"

"Yes, I saw him."

"He's following me. And I don't think he's a fan."

"Well, let me know if there is anything I can do to help."

"I will. Thanks, Father!" said Dylan, shaking hands with the priest. Then, he began walking west on Madison. He stopped at the corner of Madison and LaSalle to give one of the homeless men asking for money a $5 McDonald's gift certificate, a practice he had begun several years earlier.

He knew the rule. Don't give the homeless money for fear they may spend it on drugs or alcohol, but buying them a sandwich or providing them with a food gift card would ensure they got a meal.

"God bless you!" smiled the homeless black man, dressed in dirty and worn-out clothes, his greying hair disheveled, with patches of bristly hair across his face and neck.

"Thanks! God bless you as well! Keep the faith!" encouraged Dylan, feeling numb at the sight of the toothless man.

"Oh, I will!" he mumbled and smiled. "I will!"

Dylan's heart dropped. It was hard to see any human being in that situation, yet he knew that man was part of a growing and disturbing trend. Large numbers of homeless were now filling the streets of America due to drug and alcohol abuse, mental illness, depression, unemployment, and an economy that rejected older workers. So many of those homeless men were over fifty years old. Dylan wondered how many had been pushed out of the workforce. Or was their homelessness mostly because of depression, drugs and alcohol, as most people believed?

There were so many reasons and circumstances that resulted in citizens finding themselves out in the cold, depending on the kindness of strangers. The story of The Good Samaritan and Christ's call for all of us to "love one another as I have loved you" were always priorities for Dylan when passing by a person in need.

He tried to be prepared for those moments, but sometimes he didn't have food gift cards with him and would give the homeless person a few dollars. He knew he was breaking the rule, but he didn't have the heart to pass them by without providing some level of support.

He watched the homeless man continue shaking his paper cup of coins, seeking other donations, before venturing off to the McDonalds a few blocks away.

Dylan smiled and continued his journey home, just two miles west to his condo on Monroe. When he reached Des Plaines, however, he immediately remembered his visit to the police statue earlier that day and decided to take a detour, walking two blocks north to Randolph Street.

At Randolph, he turned left and crossed the bridge over the Kennedy Expressway. Straight in front of him was the area where the Haymarket Riot took place. After crossing the expressway overpass, Dylan knew he was standing in the exact place where the large mob of demonstrators was packed together watching Methodist minister, Samuel Fielden, atop an old wooden wagon, yelling out his speech to the mass of cold, drenched, tired, hungry and angry German-American men. Dylan tried to imagine what it must have been like on that cold and rainy night 129 years earlier. He looked across the street to see the black-canopied Haymarket Bar & Grill with the old red pickup truck in front of it. From the photos, that looked like the area where the wild-eyed minister had given his speech.

It was May 4, 1886. Workers were fed up with poor working conditions and long days. The large crowd of extremely frustrated men called for an eight-hour workday. Dylan imagined the mob shouting their support for the words of the anarchist. He could see them pumping their fists in the air with each rebellious sentence uttered by their protest leader. Then, Dylan thought some in the crowd might have glanced over their shoulders to see the police coming up the street near Halsted. The cops were lined up in three rows. Certainly, that must have made the demonstrators nervous, highly anxious! It had been a peaceful protest up until that moment, but now they were riled up, angry! And the cops looked like they were about to put an end to it.

Dylan walked to the exact spot near Halsted Street where the Chicago Police had come marching in toward the wagon, and Inspector John Bonfield had proclaimed: *"I command you in the name of the law to desist and you to disperse!"*

And as the police had moved forward toward the protestors, just a few feet in front of Dylan was where a bomb had been thrown. The front row of police must have seen it land right in front of them, the fuse burning bright on such a foggy, rainy night.

A bolt of terror must have filled those frontline cops who hadn't had time to run before the bomb exploded, sending metal shards everywhere, piercing through bodies, killing seven policemen—a horrible death!

Dylan could see in his mind's eye the mayhem that had ensued. Protestors running, police pulling out their guns and shooting, some in the mob shooting back. Gunfire everywhere!

Yelling, screaming. Horrified German and Bohemian men running in all directions, trying to escape injury, death, jail.

When it all had come to an end, just five minutes later, Dylan could imagine those dead and injured lying there on the wet and dirty orange-bricked street of Randolph, directly in front of where he was standing.

He looked over to see the spot along the curb on Randolph where he imagined the five socialist leaders of the Revenge Rally had been taken into custody by highly agitated police who must have lost all patience by that point. Dylan was sure the agitators must have been roughed up pretty well before they were thrown into the back of the police wagons. All but one would be sentenced to death by hanging, another historical moment captured in an old photograph.

History, right before his eyes! Dylan loved it! And he knew that despite the intent of the socialists and anarchists, the true purpose of the workingmen's strike against McCormick Harvester Works had been fulfilled, as their efforts led to an eight-hour workday for Americans from coast to coast.

Then, he glanced over toward the spot where the police memorial statue had stood for years. He walked over to where it had been blown up twice, spray painted and finally moved.

He envisioned a group of five long-haired, jean-jacketed, black-leather-booted, draft-card-burning hippies walking up to the statue on October 6, 1969. They placed a bomb between the policeman's legs and then ran for cover to avoid injury from the explosion. They probably jumped for joy, cheering when they saw the fragments of the sculpture flying into the air and onto the newly named Kennedy Expressway.

History!

Dylan loved revisiting historical sites like Haymarket. It made history come to life, made it real. It reminded him of the struggles men and women had endured forever. They were mostly man-made struggles—fights that could have been avoided, should never have occurred. But he knew that the battle of wills was present then, as it would be forever. People had to have their way and just couldn't get along, despite the pleas of Rodney King in Los Angeles in 1992.

Now, thanks to the efforts of Captain Panozzo's Secret Service friend in the White House, Dylan was about to step into another man-made struggle. And he hoped his prayers that day at St. Peter's would be answered.

His moment of reliving history on Randolph, between Des Plaines and Halsted, began attracting the attention of pointing pedestrians. On this hot May day, he wasn't wearing his now-famous black overcoat and gray turtleneck shirt, but he was an attractive twenty-nine-year-old who had become so famous the previous year that his face, thick wavy brown hair, blue jeans and brown Chukka boots had the attention of several in the area.

Time to go, he thought. And back toward Madison, he walked with several young men and women now running up behind him. Always seeking to be polite, he stopped for autographs and iPhone photos. A few of the young ladies handed him their phone numbers on torn pieces of paper and requested that he, "Call me!"

He smiled, nodded and turned, walking south on Halsted three blocks to Monroe. The two-mile walk back to his home gave him plenty of opportunity to think about his busy day and begin to prepare himself mentally for the dangers that he was quite certain he would face in the near future.

He felt his phone buzz and checked it. A text from Captain Panozzo.

The man I thought was an intern never worked here. We are checking how he gained access. It's a big problem!!! Glad you spotted him. We have photos and videos of him though. We'll get him. I'll be in touch.

Dylan placed his phone back in his front pants pocket. Now he had something else to worry about that night, an unknown angry man stalking him. Then, he thought about the timing of his trip to Washington the next day. It couldn't have come at a better time.

CHAPTER SIX

May was a very busy month for President Fallon, which meant Ken Hack was burning the candle at both ends. He worked to keep his team on constant alert for another attack, while continuing to investigate the White House bombing.

On the second Tuesday in May, Dylan Reilly entered the screening area in the lobby of the J. Edgar Hoover Building. After passing through the metal detectors, he saw a familiar man quickly approaching him with a bright smile across his face.

"Dylan!" greeted Hack, reaching out to shake hands with the man he hoped might be able to help him find and apprehend the group that had attacked the White House.

"Hello, Mr. Hack," smiled Dylan, shaking hands with another one of America's heroes. "Ken. Call me Ken," he insisted.

"Ken. Thanks for inviting me to help." Dylan expressed with sincere gratitude.

Dylan noticed that their exuberant greeting had drawn the attention of a few FBI-jacketed agents in the lobby, as well as that of a dozen other people who immediately recognized him. Smiles everywhere.

"Well, thank you for offering to help. We can really use you!" Hack added.

"Thanks, Ken. I'll do everything I can."

"I know you will," smiled Hack as a tall, fairly thin, older gentlemen with thinning grey hair neatly combed to the side and wearing a dark blue Armani suit, approached them.

"Oh, here is someone you need to meet," grinned Hack, turning toward the man. "Hello, Director Phillips."

"Hello, Ken," said the director, Sheldon Phillips, as he approached, reaching out to shake hands with the highly regarded Secret Service Director. "How did the interrogation go?"

"One of them wants to talk, but his associate reminded him that he is a dead man if he does," Hack informed him. "I had them brought back to their hospital rooms for more medical attention. And we are getting them a lawyer. I was hoping this would be quick, given their condition, but it may take a while before they break. They always do, especially once they get behind bars."

"I hope you're right, Ken," said Phillips, giving Dylan a strange look.

"Oh, Director, this is the man I spoke to you about on the phone the other day, Dylan Reilly," said Hack with a proud smile, happy to introduce the man famous for stopping the terrorists in Chicago the previous year. "Dylan, meet FBI Director Sheldon Phillips."

A fake, frozen smile appeared on Phillips' face. "Yes, I recognize him." The director responded in a less than welcoming fashion, because Hack had insisted that Dylan be allowed to help the effort to find the other 1917 members responsible for the attack.

"As you know, I asked him to join us. He flew in from Chicago this morning."

The director turned his full attention toward Dylan. "Well, as I told Ken and the police officer in Chicago who had initially contacted us about you, I don't think we need your help," continued Phillips in a somewhat scolding tone. "But Ken feels strongly that you will be a valuable asset to all of our efforts, so we've ironed it out and have you coordinating your efforts with Agent Jamal Gage, one of our best."

Dylan could see Hack was not too thrilled at Phillips' attitude toward the man he had personally invited in to help. A puzzled look grew on his face. "Okay, well, I want his help," Hack informed him in no uncertain terms, dropping his respectful and polite demeanor. "So he'll be working with me and Gage, and we'll try to stay out of your way."

"It's not you, Ken," blurted Phillips defensively appealing to him, hoping not to upset the nation's top Secret Service agent. "Please don't take this the wrong way. I don't want this going up the chain to the…"

"He's working with me and Agent Gage. You don't have to worry about anything else. I'll be in touch."

"That's fine," voiced Phillips somewhat nervously, now quite sure that he had offended the man whom President Fallon had publicly stated he counted on most to protect his life.

"C'mon, Dylan, I need to go back to the White House, and I'd like you to join me," requested Hack, glaring at Phillips as he began leading his new teammate out the door.

"Thanks, Ken, I appreciate it," said Dylan, nodding at Phillips as he walked past him.

"Absolutely!" feigned Phillips, who was probably then considering the negative press coverage the FBI, and he in particular, would receive if it became public that he had attempted to reject the help offered by Dylan Reilly.

The two American heroes walked out the glass doors of the FBI building. Hack seemed most eager to hear Dylan's perspective on the terrorist attack. "Dylan, do you have any ideas about what you think we should do next?" he asked, sounding eager for some great ideas, given his failed interrogation that morning.

"I do. I absolutely do," Dylan informed him with great enthusiasm.

Just then, Hack's phone buzzed. He glanced at the text.

"C'mon, let's hurry. The President needs us now."

Off they ran toward the parking garage as passersby noticed and began pointing at the man from Chicago who had dominated news coverage a year earlier to become a household name.

CHAPTER SEVEN

Entering the apartment complex in western D.C., the FedEx delivery man didn't seem to draw the attention of the three rough-looking white men exiting the elevator. But when he passed, the taller man, who was speaking Russian to his two friends, turned to take another look.

Nothing.

He turned back and proceeded, continuing his conversation in Russian with a dialect from Moscow.

Dylan Reilly's disguise worked wonderfully. Unshaven, with his hair tucked under a blue cap and dressed in a FedEx shirt and blue pants, he carried a white box into the elevator and up to the third floor. His Smith and Wesson six-shooter was hidden nicely under his navy blue shirt, purposely not tucked inside his pants in order to conceal his weapon.

When the elevator doors opened, he searched for apartment 316. A few moments later, he knocked at the door, mentally prepared for anything that might occur once it opened. He saw the peephole darken. Was that one of the members of the 1917 terror group now looking at him, he wondered.

The door opened.

"Yes!" blurted a short, thin, long-bearded man wearing a black t-shirt, black cargo pants and black combat boots. He looked like he had fallen out of *Soldier of Fortune* magazine.

"Got a package for you," Dylan revealed, handing the man the electronic signature device to sign. As he signed it, he peered up at Dylan, trying to confirm in his own mind that he was indeed a FedEx driver. He handed the electronic signature pad back to him.

"I thought they got rid of these signature devices," said the man in a somewhat accusatory tone of voice.

"We only have to get a signature when it's requested by the seller of a valuable item," he explained, hoping the stern-faced man would buy it.

"I see," he said, then looked back over his shoulder, giving Dylan a chance to see inside the open door. He had a full view of three men sitting at a table in the kitchen area. They were rough-looking characters, probably in their early thirties, with shoulder-length hair and long beards on their big, ugly faces. They, too, were dressed in black, just like the man answering the door. There were two guns on the counter, a Glock and AR-15.

"Well thank you sir," said Dylan, extending the package out to the man, who turned back to accept it. One of the men at the table noticed Dylan looking inside the apartment. His eyes narrowed.

"Yeah, great," said the man at the door, looking at the package, then up at Dylan who realized that it was time to high-tail it out of there, if he didn't want to get into a shooting match with this group, whom he hoped to expose as 1917 members, linked to the White House attack.

He ran down the hall quickly, pressed the elevator button, then ducked through the door of the staircase just to the right, running quickly down the stairs. As the door closed behind him, he could hear someone running in the hall. Then, he heard the elevator doors open.

"Hey, there's no one in the elevator! Where did he go?"

"I don't know. Maybe he had another delivery."

"That's not a delivery man, stupid! You go that way. I'll check the stairs."

In less than a minute, Dylan flew down three flights of stairs. He could hear someone running down the steps above him. Not fast enough, though.

He was out the door and into a blinding sunlight, turning left and clinging to the front of the building, so he couldn't be spotted from above. At the corner of the building, he took off fast, sprinting about one hundred yards to the black FBI Suburban waiting for him. He jumped into the open side door, and the vehicle sped off.

Looking out the back window, he could see the man who had answered the door running outside of the building. He stopped and searched the area. Nothing. Then, he looked in the direction of the black SUV speeding off and placed his hands on his hips in frustration.

"Was it them?" asked Agent Jamal Gage, who had been assigned to work with Dylan on the reconnaissance mission.

"It was definitely someone up to no good," informed Dylan, huffing and puffing, still trying to catch his breath from the long run down the stairs. "There was an assault weapon and a Glock gun on the kitchen counter. The guy who answered the door kept eyeballing me, not trusting I was with FedEx. There were three others inside, and one noticed that I spotted the guns. They came out after me in the hallway, but I went down the stairs."

"Smart!" acknowledged Gage, a well-built, six-foot-tall African American agent who had been with the Bureau for twenty years, since graduating from Georgetown University, where he had come off the bench as a point guard on the basketball team. He had grown up in D.C., in the projects, very close to area they had just left.

He knew at the age of fourteen that he was going to become an FBI agent, after falling in love with the show *FBI*, starring Efrem Zimbalist Jr., which he had happened to find in reruns. He was the type of agent who rolled out of bed every day excited to go to work at the J. Edgar Hoover Building on Pennsylvania Avenue.

"Thanks! So I've got his signature here," Dylan informed him, handing Gage the electronic pad.

"Ivan Henry," he revealed, unfamiliar with that name. "Never heard of him."

"Could be an alias," admitted Dylan.

"Could be," Gage agreed, trying to recall if he had ever come across the name before. He had a great memory for names, especially those of criminals.

Just as the powerful Chevy Suburban pulled into the parking lot at FBI Headquarters, Gage received a call. "Yes!" He listened. "Oh, no! Okay. We're back now. We'll be right up."

"They've got Hack's wife," he informed Dylan with a great look of concern on his face.

"Damn!" cursed Dylan, clenching his teeth. Then, he thought about that revelation for a moment. "How could they know Hack is involved?"

"Good question," Gage agreed, pointing at him. "How could they know?"

A few minutes later, they were back up in the conference room, where Director Sheldon Phillips and Gary Stein, Director of the Operational Technology Division, were waiting for them.

"What happened?" Gage asked, hoping his boss would have more encouraging news.

"We just got a call from an anonymous source telling us they want Hack, or they'll kill his wife," Phillips explained. "This is Gary Stein, head of our technical division. The call was cut off before we could trace it."

Stein interrupted. "Yes, but we were able to get a three-square-mile radius of the area they were calling from. It's right in the same neighborhood you just came from."

"We didn't see anyone in the…"

"No, I don't think that's where they brought her," explained Phillips. "But we think she's being held somewhere around there."

"Does Hack know?" asked Dylan, concerned for his new friend, whom he had quickly grown to respect for his integrity, courage and commitment to the country.

"He's on his way over now," said Phillips, shaking his head, obviously thinking of how Hack would respond to such a horrible situation.

"So what are we going to do?" asked Gage.

"Well, we had better wait to see what Ken has to say. We still have those two in the holding area, so we do have some leverage."

"Director, how could they possibly know Ken Hack was involved?" asked Gage.

"That's a good question," Stein announced. "I've been wondering that myself."

"Well however they found out, we've now got a serious problem we have to resolve," Phillips alerted them, with a note of great concern in his voice.

"Do we know where they are?" asked a very upset Ken Hack, exploding through the door. "I've got to get Elizabeth out of there. I don't care what it takes."

"Okay, Ken, I know you're upset, but let's take this a step at a time," Phillips stated firmly. "Dylan, I want you to meet with Gary's team and give them a description of the men you saw in the apartment. Did we get a signature?"

"Yes!" confirmed Agent Gage. "His name is Ivan Henry. I never heard of him."

"Me, neither!" admitted Phillips. "Gary, can you run that through the system to see what you come up with?"

"Will do. And Ken, can you join us?" Stein asked. "I've got some information I want to go over with you from the attack that I think may help us."

"Absolutely," offered Hack. "How much time are they giving us on this?"

"They will be calling back this afternoon with further instructions," Phillips revealed. "We've got surveillance vans in the area that may be able to pick up the signal quicker and help us locate them once they call."

"I hope so," said Hack. "But if it's Elizabeth or me, I'm going."

"Ken, I've got an idea," Dylan interjected, trying to provide hope. "And you're just the guy that can help me pull it off."

Hack now looked at his new pal, who was providing him with a much-needed sliver of hope. He was well aware of what Dylan had done in the past. He would need some of that magic to get his wife back safe and unharmed.

CHAPTER EIGHT

It was a peaceful Sunday, a morning when it seemed everything was right in the world.

The sky was blue. The sun shined brightly onto the tall spire of St. Anthony's church in central Florida, as the sound of the organ bellowed out of two large, open oak front doors. The voices of the three hundred parishioners poured out, woven into the rising musical prayer.

Reverent and faithful families filled the pews. Mothers stood next to daughters wearing pretty, colorful and respectable mid-length summer dresses. Fathers and sons were dressed neatly in polo shirts, shorts and sandals. Twenty-something singles, along with some graying and white-haired widows and widowers, were scattered throughout the beautifully decorated church. Middle-aged Baby Boomers, mostly women, were seated with their elderly parents, the wheelchairs parked at the ends of the pews.

A large cross with the bloodied crucified Jesus hung from the ceiling, with two long metal cables securely holding it in place. The shadow of Christ on the cross fell onto the bright white marble altar table, with tall golden candlestick holders on each side and a golden tabernacle centered behind the altar. It was most certainly a church where donations from committed parishioners helped to support a very impressive display of sacred objects.

Father Lawrence O'Leary had just finished his homily on Ecclesiastes 10: 8-9, which said: *Whoever digs a pit may fall into it; Whoever breaks through a wall may be bitten by a snake. Whoever quarries stones may be injured by them; whoever splits logs may be endangered by them.*

As the congregation sat contemplating the meaning of the Bible verse and Father O'Leary's analysis, which encouraged them to be careful about their wishes and the actions taken to achieve their dreams, because those choices might come back to bite them in the end.

A few minutes later, the priest stood behind the altar table, preparing for the sacred blessing. A middle-aged, balding deacon stood to his right. Father O'Leary held the Host in front of him, saying, "On the night He was betrayed, He took bread and gave you thanks and praise. He broke the bread, gave it to His disciples and said, 'Take this all of you and eat it. This is my Body, which will be given up for you.'"

Father O'Leary raised the Host high, staring up toward heaven. A freckled-faced twelve-year-old altar boy kneeling on the bright blue carpet at the foot of the altar rang the bells three times. He watched the priest enact the holy moment known as transubstantiation, when the bread became the body of Christ.

All eyes were focused on this holy and reverent act, knowing they were reliving the moment at the Last Supper, when Jesus gave His twelve apostles the most sacred of Christian traditions. He wanted them to take it out into the world and build His Church, letting believers know that He was alive.

As Father O'Leary lowered his arms, his focus was interrupted by the sound of screeching tires from outside the church. The forty-year-old priest wondered if there had been an accident. He shook his head, not wishing to disturb the holy moment. He then took the golden chalice and began reciting, "In a similar way, when supper was ended, He took the cup. Again, He gave you thanks and praise..."

Just then, four men dressed in tan camouflage military fatigues and carrying assault rifles entered the church. As the priest raised the chalice, he immediately saw them. His eyes grew wide. His mouth dropped. He finished the prayer. "Do this in memory of me."

At that moment, bullets were sprayed across the altar. The priest, hit several times, fell back and to the floor. The chalice flew up in the air, and the Blood of Christ soaked into the blue carpet. The young altar boy lay on the altar carpet, bleeding and in tremendous pain. The deacon was dead, shot through the head.

Screams filled the sanctuary. Parishioners tried to run for their lives. All four terrorists opened up with their AR-15 semiautomatic rifles, shooting everyone in sight. Mothers in their once-pretty bright dresses fell to the ground, covered in blood. Young girls shot, bleeding, crying for help. Fathers and sons lay dead on the floor. A few men tried charging the killers and were mercilessly shot down, the rat-a-tat-tat sound of the machine gun-like rifles bouncing off the walls of God's House.

One of the killers, who was holding a large canvas bag, walked up to the altar and grabbed the golden candlesticks, tabernacle and chalice and shoved them into his bag. His associate, the leader of this vicious group, held a machete in his right hand. He walked over to the statue of Mary and, with one swing, chopped her head off. He walked around the entire church, chopping every statue in half. A tall, ugly, strong-looking man followed him, throwing gasoline onto the broken statues, then setting them aflame.

The leader walked up to the critically injured priest, who lay bleeding on the carpet. He looked down at him and announced, "We are going to kill every Catholic, break every statue, burn every church, mutilate every priest. We will destroy the Catholic Church! We will destroy America!"

He then lifted his machete up high and with all of his might, chopped down on the priest's neck, decapitating him. From the great force of the thrust, his head rolled a few feet over the wine-soaked carpet. It was a horrific image of a Catholic martyr's death.

The four murderers walked down the center aisle toward the open door, pouring out their gas cans. They stepped over bloody corpses, shooting anyone still breathing. Just a few minutes earlier, a church filled with happy, faithful Christians now presented a scene of death, blood and mayhem.

These sadistic killers, who looked to be in their mid-thirties—

rough-looking, hardened men—stood outside the entrance of the church. Their leader raised his rifle and fired bullets into the two gasoline cans left in the main aisle. Fire shot up from the red metal containers and quickly spread across the entire sanctuary.

Watching the devastation, they laughed, high-fived each other while walking to the two black Humvees parked in front of the church.

"I wish Dmitri could be here to see this," snickered one of them.

Another responded, "Oh, he will. I recorded it on my phone."

"Good thinking. He'll love it."

They drove off as fire alarms rang out from inside the burning sanctuary. The fire department would be there soon. Not soon enough, though, to save any of the lives on the floor of St. Anthony's church.

The beautiful day had turned into a day of terror and death.

CHAPTER NINE

A battered and bloodied Elizabeth Hack sat on a beige metal folding chair, her arms duct taped together behind her back. Her legs were tied tightly together with a white rope around her ankles. Tears poured down her beautiful olive-skinned cheeks. Her long brown hair lay disheveled atop her head from the abuse; some had fallen across her face, partially blocking her vision.

"Don't worry, lady. Once we get your husband here, we'll let you go," laughed a tall, thin, unusually clean terrorist with a full head of gray hair combed to the side and impeccably dressed in tight black jeans, a black shirt and new cargo boots. "Did you hear that, comrades? We'll let her go, won't we?"

The three other men in the room, all younger, all wearing black, laughed loudly, then watched their leader reach back and slap the woman hard across the face.

Her anger and disdain grew as she turned back to her captor. "Oh, you're a real tough guy, aren't you?" a defiant Elizabeth Hack yelled out. "Beating a woman tied up. If you cut this tape off and let me fight back, then we'd find out how tough you are!"

"Oooooh." A chorus of derision echoed through the kitchen at the challenge to the leader of this anarchist group, determined to bring down America. His initial plan had failed, but the mission would go on. Before moving forward, however, he was going to exact revenge on the man who had killed his three talented 1917 members in President's Park.

One of the other men, the shortest of the group and prematurely gray, walked up to Elizabeth, bent down and looked her right in the eyes. "Are you tough, lady?" he asked, then took his knife out and cut her blue skirt up the middle, tearing it off with a hard tug, leaving her sitting in her pink underwear. "Oh, look at this, boys! How about we take her in the bedroom and…?"

"Okay, Frank, you idiot!" yelled Ivan Henry, stopping his three comrades from continuing. "You'll have your fun later. But right now, we need to stay focused on getting Hack here. Just because we have his pretty little wife doesn't mean we have him."

"What time did you tell them he had to be here?" asked Frank Pestola, a short, bald, frumpy-looking thirty-five-year-old loser wearing large black-rimmed glasses.

"By two p.m., or we will cut her throat!" vowed Henry, sending a shiver through the olive-skinned Italian American beauty. "They've got thirty minutes to bring him to the other apartment."

Two blocks away, in apartment 316 at Brentland Manor, the four other members of Henry's team waited for Hack to arrive. One peered out the window, expecting some vehicle to pull up with the White House Secret Service agent. The other three sat at the kitchen table with guns at the ready.

Dylan and Hack were positioned in the window across the street. Hack had his sniper Winchester Magnum arranged in the best position to take out as many as possible of the enemy confined in the fairly small quarters. He was surprised to see they had left the window shades up, which allowed him to see the four men inside at the table. He could see one of them talking on a cell phone, while another looked out the window.

The lookout wouldn't be able to spot Hack, who had kept the blinds drawn, with an opening just large enough to see through his rifle sight. The man looking out the window was looking down, as if he expected to see someone, or something, on the street below.

"Dylan, they are looking for someone below," informed Hack, who could hear the phone buzzing in his earpiece. Stein had set up a direct feed between himself, Hack and Phillips back at headquarters. As directed by Hack, Stein controlled when all three were on the line and when he could cut off Phillips, whom Hack was uncertain he could trust.

"Yes," said Phillips, answering the call being fed to Hack and Stein.

"Where is Hack?" barked Henry in a belligerent tone. "Would you like to see his wife, because if he isn't here in the next five minutes, it's the last you will ever see of her. Understood?"

He then pointed his phone toward Elizabeth Hack. The Facetime call showed her badly beaten face, covered with tears and sitting in her underwear. Ken Hack's head was about to explode, he was so angry. He held his temper, knowing one word from him could result in her death.

"Beautiful, isn't she?" sneered Henry. "Oh, don't worry. We will have our fun with her first, before we kill her."

"Hack's on his way. Don't kill her. You'll get what you want!" Phillips pleaded, hoping to buy time from the demented man on the other end of the line.

"Well, your time is running out, Director. You know where to bring him—the same place you sent that fake FedEx delivery man to the other day. Two minutes. You've got only two minutes."

"Let me just ask you…"

"No! No more questions! Get him here!" Henry demanded, ending the call, knowing the time limit on tracing, or at least what he thought was the time limit.

"Damn! He hung up!" cursed Phillips. "Stein, did we trace it?"

"We're checking, sir," explained Stein, who at that moment was sending a text to Hack, just as he had been instructed by him.

Hack saw a text pop up from Stein.

I got 'em! 1422 Saratoga. Right here the building next door. 302! 302! Third floor!

Hack swung his large, powerful weapon around to 1422, then up three floors. And there they were. "I got 'em, Dylan. Go! Go!"

Out the door Dylan bolted, and within seconds, it seemed, Hack saw him sprint across the street up to the 1422 building. Hack glanced back at the other apartment, and the lookout had spotted Dylan running.

"Damn!" cursed Hack, then texted Dylan.

The lookout spotted you running across the street. They'll probably be ready for you when you get there.

While Dylan ran up the stairs, he glanced at the text. Okay, no problem, he thought.

Hack looked through his gun sight and scanned the apartment. A tall grey-haired man was pacing back and forth. That was the moment he saw his wife.

"You're dead! Every one of you!" he shouted out, forgetting he was still live on the linked-in feed to Stein.

"Ken!" exclaimed Stein. "Are you okay?"

"Oh, yes. Sorry, Gary," he apologized. "I forgot I was still on here. They've got my wife tied up, and she's beaten up pretty badly. I'm going to get every last one of them!"

"We're with you, Ken. We will keep tracking this. Good luck!"

"Thanks," he responded with appreciation, continuing to move his sight around to see as much as he could inside the apartment, hoping to give Dylan as much information as possible.

The tall gray-haired man who had been on the phone disappeared out of his view, but Hack could see the other men, dressed in black, moving around. Hack's sure-fire ability would allow him to take down two immediately. He held his fire, though, until Dylan arrived, giving them both a better chance to take out all of the terrorists and save Elizabeth.

"Ken, are you on your way to the apartment?" asked Phillips. Stein could hear him and opened up the three-way line again.

"Repeat, please," Stein requested.

"Ken, are you on your way?" asked Phillips, sounding panicked.

"In motion," informed Hack, obviously not willing to trust anyone at Headquarters.

"Okay, well, get there quick," directed Phillips. "There's only two minutes left."

"Will do, sir," he acknowledged, as Stein cut Phillips' connection off again.

"Just you and me, Ken," said Stein.

"Great! Thanks, Gary. This is going to happen in the next couple minutes, so just stay on the line."

"Will do."

Hack got ready behind his trusty 300 Winchester Magnum. He then watched Henry take another call.

"Gary, are you still connected to Phillips?"

"Yes, why?"

"You're sure?"

"One hundred percent. He's still on the line."

Hack watched Henry point toward the door. The terrorists in the other apartment had called, after seeing Dylan run across the street. Hack watched as the other men inside, each armed with a semiautomatic weapon, pointed toward the entrance.

Henry sent the dimwitted Frank Pestola to answer the door. If he were shot, it would be no loss. Pestola looked through the peephole and saw a UPS man with a package.

"It's UPS," he announced, turning to his comrades. As he turned, Dylan kicked in the door, pulled out his six-shooter and started unloading on Pestola and then Henry, right behind him. At the same time, bullets broke through the window, taking out the two other socialists positioned to the side. Within a matter of seconds, all four terrorists were dead.

Dylan moved quickly over to Elizabeth Hack.

"Are you okay?" he asked, noticing that she had recognized him.

"Yes, I'm fine. Thank you so much!"

"Just helping your husband save the lady he loves most in this life," Dylan smiled, while cutting the duct tape off of her hands and the rope around her ankles.

"Aren't you—you know, that guy who..."

"Yeah, I'm the guy."

Elizabeth rose and threw her arms around him, giving him a hug for saving her life. "Thank you so much!" she cried, tears pouring down her cheeks.

Dylan grabbed his phone. "I got her, Ken!" he informed the fearful husband.

"Thank God! Thank God!" a greatly relieved Ken Hack shared, thanking his new pal. "I'll keep an eye out for the other group. They may be coming. Just be careful getting out of there, Dylan."

"Will do. I'll meet you at the truck."

Dylan quickly found a quilted blanket on the beat-up old gold couch and handed it to Elizabeth, whose dress was beyond repair.

"C'mon, we got to go!" he pronounced, leading her out the front door, his six-shooter at the ready. The coast was clear. When they reached ground level, he glanced over at the other apartment and saw four men running toward him.

Making certain to stay out of the line of fire, in case they had a sniper positioned on the top floor, he led Elizabeth along the front of the building and took a hard left to take cover.

He peeked around the corner of the building and could see the four men, all dressed in black, with balaclavas over their heads, and each carrying an AK-15 semiautomatic weapon. They spotted Dylan and Elizabeth. The leader pointed for two of them to go behind the building to cut off Dylan's escape.

Realizing their plan, Dylan would need Ken's help one more time.

"Ken, do you see those two out front?" he asked over the dedicated line.

"I got 'em," Ken confirmed confidently.

"Okay, I'll take the two coming around the back."

Dylan had Elizabeth stand inside a doorway where she would have cover, then walked toward the back of the building.

The two men running in front of the building were like ducks on a pond for Hack, still positioned in his sniper's nest on the top floor of the building across the street.

A shot rang out. Down went the first 1917 killer, the one who had been the lookout. The man behind him stopped and looked back at the apartment building where he believed the shot must have come from. He turned his weapon toward the top floor, but before he could squeeze the trigger, blam! The bullet tore through his right shoulder. He fell backwards, screaming in pain. His weapon flew up in the air and landed on the ground next to him. He reached over to grab it when, blam! A bullet pierced through his left shoulder.

Like the kid in President's Park, Hack wasn't going to kill him. They would need him for questioning.

At the same time, the two remaining from the 1917 gang came running around the building to find a UPS man with a holster around his waist and a six-shooter in the holster.

Shock filled their face as they stopped running, still twenty-five yards away from Dylan.

"Who the hell is that?" one of them asked, thinking perhaps his associate might know.

"I don't know, but you can ask him when he's lying dead on the ground," predicted the other man with an evil look in his eyes, raising his weapon directly at Dylan.

Before he could squeeze the trigger, Dylan drew his six-shooter with lightning-fast speed, shooting the man right between his two evil eyes.

The other man watched him drop to the ground. Then, he looked back at Dylan and dropped his weapon. Dylan approached him with gun pointed.

"Are you the guy?" he asked, after seeing the remarkable display of speed that the whole world knew was possessed by only one man.

"Yeah, I'm the guy," Dylan confirmed, picking up the man's

weapon and leading him back to the front of the building. The sound of sirens once again filled the air.

As Dylan led his prisoner to the front of the building, he watched a familiar armored SWAT vehicle screech up to the scene. Five battle-ready officers jumped out with Colt M4 Carbines, looking for any other would-be assailants.

Commander Dirk Williams jumped out of the truck and approached Ken Hack, who had hustled down and was hugging his wife, so happy she had made it out alive.

It was a happy moment on a day that could have been tragic.

CHAPTER TEN

It was the final Tuesday of May. The temperature in Chicago had skyrocketed to 90 degrees. Across the downtown campus of CIU, it was a summer scene.

A stream of colorful youth paraded through the Lecture Center Plaza. College guys were dressed in shorts and t-shirts, while the young ladies wore culottes, light casual tops, and summer dresses.

Marty Mahoney, an eighteen-year-old from the Mount Greenwood neighborhood on Chicago's southwest side, was one of them. He was preparing to start his freshman year at CIU, with the hopes of becoming a lawyer.

The thin, red-headed Mahoney had been a straight A student and cross-country star at St. John's Academy in the southwest suburbs. He had chosen CIU in order to stay close to home. He wasn't accustomed to attending school during the summer but didn't see the point of waiting.

During his first few days on the campus, he saw a group of students milling about a table set up on the plaza. A large sign reading "RESIST" stood to the side of the table where dozens of students had lined up.

Curious, he walked over to check it out. He quickly learned that students were being asked to sign a petition calling for stricter accountability among Chicago Police officers. This was coming after months of news stories trying to ascertain the truth about an unarmed teenage boy being shot by a veteran police officer who patrolled the very dangerous South Side Englewood neighborhood. When a videotape of the shooting had become public, a series of protests had been held, calling on Chicago's mayor, Rahm Emanuel, to demand much stricter accountability.

Those pleas hadn't lasted long, after an independent journalist had blown the lid off of a major cover-up being orchestrated by Mayor Emanuel. Through a lawsuit, freelance journalist Brandon Smith had attained the right to view a videotape from a police-cam which showed the shooting of the unarmed teenager.

For months, Emanuel had kept information about the video out of the public eye and then dodged the allegations that he led the cover-up. Once the truth came out and all of the other media outlets picked up on Smith's story, Emanuel realized that he had lost all credibility with the voters and dropped out of the upcoming race to keep his job at City Hall.

But the rage and anger created by the shooting and the city government's attempt to hide information motivated a lot of young people to join various advocacy groups that had organized protests calling for accountability in the police force. The black community was especially upset, given it had been another unarmed black youth who had been shot and killed by a police officer. They argued that the boy was no angel, but he hadn't deserved to be shot and killed.

Marty Mahoney had grown up in a neighborhood filled with Chicago cops and fire fighters. His family knew dozens of those first responders, and they were always supportive.

They didn't view the shooting incident as a widespread issue, but the irresponsible act of one bad cop who didn't represent the good work being done by thousands of great cops.

Despite the constant negatively slanted and politically correct news stories that followed, painting all the police as the bad guys, most people living in Marty's neighborhood respected and appreciated the cops who were putting their lives on the line for the citizens of the city on a daily basis.

They knew that nearly all of those men and women in blue were heroes, not the bad guys being portrayed by some in the news media.

They knew that most of the protestors didn't have a full understanding of the reality of the issue, including the history between the police and black citizens on the south and west sides of Chicago.

It was long and violent past, resulting from poor living conditions, family instability and the evolution of gangs selling drugs in order to make money. With so much money at stake, turf wars and vengeful shootings had occurred for several decades, going back to the 1960s.

This was not new but had escalated greatly in the new Millennium. The cops who had to police those neighborhoods on a daily basis, who were trying to bring some form of social order, had to be courageous to take on such an assignment, while receiving low pay and little respect.

That was the point of debate that had begun with the incident on South Pulaski Road and would continue across the country for years to come.

On this hot Tuesday at CIU, that debate was top of mind for Marty as he walked past the table, glancing down at the petition. He turned and thumbed in the information on the sign, set next to the table, promoting attendance at a protest on Lake Shore Drive later that week.

As someone who wanted to become a prosecutor for the Illinois State's Attorney's Office, Marty thought he would attend the rally to see how protests were run, who attended them, and what they actually accomplished.

The two students behind the table saw him typing into his phone.

"Hey, you should sign the petition, man!" exclaimed Rob Slagle, the long-dark-haired hipster who had been ordered by the socialist leader Wooten to sign up as many students from CIU as possible. The redheaded Irish freshman just smiled, waved politely and walked toward his next class.

"Yeah, we gotta stop these cops from killing us, especially our black brothers, man!" yelled out Tim Kamus, one of Wooten's other socialist soldiers, trying to encourage Marty to sign.

"Hey, man, you're either with us or against us!" yelled out the hipster.

Marty stopped. He turned and smirked at the kid trying to manipulate him with that threat. Mahoney wasn't the biggest or strongest eighteen-year-old in the city. He was thin, built like the cross-country star he had become at St. John's Academy. Despite his size, he would never shy away from a fight. He looked back at the hipster, who could see Mahoney was ready to fight and quickly backed off, sitting back down. Marty shook his head and continued on to class.

A few days later, Mahoney stood on the sidewalk on Fullerton Avenue, just west of Lake Shore Drive. It was a hot and muggy afternoon, but the strong wind off the lake kept things refreshingly cool.

Marty watched the protestors, each holding a sign, repeat the chant of the long-haired thirty-something at the front of the pack of nearly a hundred college students. Some of them he recognized from school, especially the hipster and balding guy at the signup table. They were standing at the front, supporting the chants of their long-haired leader.

The messages on the signs varied and revealed the talented artists versus the scribblers. Most called for an end to police abuse.

Marty hoped all Americans could support the rights and lives of all people, regardless of their race, creed or color. As stated in the Declaration of Independence:

"We hold these truths to be self-evident, that all men are created equal, that they are endowed by their Creator with certain unalienable Rights, that among these are Life, Liberty and the pursuit of Happiness."

Most of the protestors supported BLM because they believed in the slogan that "black lives matter" and believed that all Americans should be treated equal, regardless of race. However, after a quick read of the BLM website, Mahoney knew the organization itself supported a lot more than the value of all black lives. They supported communism and the evil philosophy of Karl Marx.

Marty wondered how many of the protestors had actually taken the time to read the mission of BLM. And, if they had read it, whether they would still have been out there supporting the group. He believed most probably would, but none of them would come from his neighborhood or group of friends, where the traditional values of faith and family were still the priority.

The protest began at 4:30 that afternoon, and there didn't seem to be much exuberance among the students, who were going to attempt to shut down Lake Shore Drive during rush hour.

Perhaps when that idea was floated by them earlier in the day, it may have sounded like a great idea. It would really get Chicago's attention, especially the attention of the news media.

But once the students had marched up the road leading to a very busy highway and seen cars buzzing by them at sixty to seventy miles per hour, had stepping out onto the very busy expressway to block traffic still seemed like a great idea?

Marty noticed that many of the protestors, standing on the Chicago Park District grass along the west side of Lake Shore Drive, were just going through the motions, with no real energy behind their chants. Most were taking selfies to share on their social media, so their friends would all know they were politically active, and perhaps more importantly, politically correct. Their courage had parameters set around what they could, and could not, promote to their friends via social media. Oh, they were prepared to make courageous statements and take courageous actions, as long as their friends and the social media police approved.

At 4:50 p.m., their lack of interest ended as everyone in the group watched five television news vans pull up to the scene, parking their vehicles on the grass south of Fullerton Street. The camera operators and reporters jumped out of their white vans, complete with colorful station logos on the side, ready to cover the protest. Once the crowd saw the media arrive, the energy and vocal enthusiasm of the group skyrocketed. They were going to be on TV!

The brown-bearded, long-haired leader yelled through his megaphone, "Black lives matter! Black lives matter!" And a chorus of "Black lives matter" chants was bellowed from all in the protest group, which included five black students, by Marty's count.

Mahoney watched the leader. Once he noticed that the light on each station's camera was not lit, he realized they were not being filmed. It wasn't five o'clock. The live news shows wouldn't start for another five minutes, when each station would go live to their reporters on Lake Shore Drive. So leader Longhair held his arms up to stop the chants and save his group's collective energy for their fifteen minutes of fame, when the camera lights were turned on.

In the meantime, the reporters approached students in the crowd, trying to find someone to go on camera for a live interview. Some backed away, while others pushed forward, ready for their close-up, Mr. DeMille.

Marty watched the hipster and tall guy from the CIU signup table each making their case to TV news reporters. They were dismissed. Another fellow was moving around the crowd with them, a large-headed, bulging-eyed twenty-something wearing a white-collared shirt and khaki pants. Marty thought that unusual dress for a protest, but there was no standard fashion on display, with many protestors dressed in a cacophony of clothing choices. Nonetheless, the bulging-eyed fellow was successful in getting the reporter from WMAQ-TV to interview him. He smiled toward Slagle and Kamus and gave the thumbs-up.

They looked happy to see him go on camera, obviously to promote their messages, whatever they might be.

Marty thought about walking over to hear the interview, but then saw a reporter from WBBM-TV approach Longhair. After a quick discussion, it looked like he was going to be making an appearance on the CBS station. The other reporters from WGN-TV,

WMAQ-TV, WLS-TV and WFLD-TV each found someone to interview.

Mahoney was most interested in what the leader of the pack was going to say and walked as close as possible to hear that interview. He checked his phone. Five o'clock. All at once, a bright white light appeared on each of the five news cameras, ready to deliver a live interview to their respective stations, leading off the newscasts.

With blue skies above, the sun was bright and beating down on the beautiful Hispanic reporter, Tai Martinez, who was squinting as she asked her questions.

"We gotta stop these cops!" blurted out Longhair, loud enough for Mahoney to easily hear. "We gotta defund the police! We don't need police anymore!"

"I thought you were here for Black Lives Matter?" Martinez asked, a puzzled look now apparent on her face, as the strong lake wind had its way with her long black hair.

"Oh, yeah. We support Black Lives Matter. Sure, they gotta stop killing black people, too. But we gotta get rid of the cops! We don't need 'em!"

Martinez pulled her microphone away from Longhair. She was now thoroughly confused about the protest. She turned toward the camera. "Well, as you have just heard from the leader of the protest, Mr. Chester Walling, it sounds like he is more interested in defunding the police than defending black lives. Not sure how he ended up leading this group, but we will talk with him in a minute and get the entire story for the ten p.m. newscast. Back to you, Rob."

Like Martinez, Mahoney didn't understand what he had just heard during the interview. Why was Longhair Chester Walling leading the protest? And how was it tied to the student group at CIU? None of it made any sense. He was easily in his early thirties and most likely not a student at the school. And no chance he could be a teacher, Marty thought.

He watched the other four camera lights go off as they finished their interviews as well. He watched the hipster and tall guy walk up to Mr. Bulging-Eyes and give him the all-too-familiar fist bump and half-hug. The apparently were happy with the interview.

When the news vans pulled away, it was apparent that most of the protestors were also ready to leave.

They had their moment on live television, which they would talk about for years with their family and friends. And if some black lives were saved because of their efforts, well that was just fine, too. But the headline for them was: "We Were On TV!!"

When Marty returned to Mt. Greenwood around seven that evening, he stopped at one of his older brother Pat's favorite neighborhood watering holes, Lawlor's Bar. Pat and four of his pals were sitting shoulder to shoulder at the bar, having a loud discussion between sips of their favorite draft. When Marty approached, he knew immediately that they had watched the coverage of the protest. At once, the five half-inebriated political analysts swiveled around to face him, each holding a cold mug of beer.

For the next two hours, the discussion between Marty and the neighborhood boys centered on the protestors and who was leading the students in their rebellion against the police.

Pat and his friends were glued to every word from the redhead about what he had seen and heard on the lakefront that evening. It was the inside story.

All wanted to know, who was this longhaired thirty-something, Chester Walling? And were the students being used by some radical leftist group? Those were the questions.

As Marty stood sipping his Pepsi, those questions ate at him. After watching the ridiculous protest that afternoon, he was determined to find out for himself.

CHAPTER ELEVEN

Director Phillips paced the floor of his plush office, his hands clasped behind his back, pondering the very serious situation. The previous day, he had met with President Fallon and Attorney General Edward Crandell, who had placed a great deal of pressure on him to find and stop the organization responsible for the domestic terrorist attacks that were taking place across the country. The President promised to commit any resources Phillips needed to get the job done, including sending the National Guard.

"We can't allow terrorists to massacre our citizens!" Crandell stated at a packed news conference held in Washington. "For those cowardly criminals who orchestrated such a vile act, murdering three hundred and five innocent people inside St. Anthony's, the United States government will find you and bring you to justice."

News of the massacre at the church in Florida sent shock waves through the country. In the past, there had been attacks on churches, with violent killings, but those had been conducted by lone individuals. Angry men! Nuts! This had been orchestrated by a trained and experienced group on a major scale. It was horrific! And Americans were scared.

Phillips knew he would have to depend heavily on his surveillance team, if he was going to find and apprehend all of the members of this group. The problem was that he didn't know how many terror cells there were, where they were located, and who was funding them.

Stein entered the director's office holding his open Mac laptop in his right hand.

"We found a socialist group in Chicago that is actively involved in the demonstrations there!" he informed Phillips, trying to show him the North Side location on his computer. "They are blending in with the Black Lives Matter demonstrators. But according to one news report from the CBS station, the leader of the protest was more interested in bringing down America and the police than supporting BLM. We have audio, video, and the news report for you to see."

Phillips gave Stein a puzzled look and raised his hands in dismay. "What about Florida?" he asked, knowing that was the directive he had given Stein and his group. He was expecting some lead on the group that had the country on edge.

"We are still working on that, sir," Stein explained. "We're getting closer, so don't worry. We'll get it. We always do."

"I hope so," said Phillips with more than a note of disappointment in his voice. "That's the priority for the President. He is under great criticism from the press for not having the perpetrators of that attack identified and stopped. The President and Attorney General Edward Crandell have now placed responsibility for finding them squarely on my shoulders."

Stein paused a moment, trying to give his director time to calm down. He stood there watching Phillips start to pace again. "Sir, there is a protest planned tomorrow in Chicago. I'd like to dispatch our local team to work with our asset there and infiltrate the group, find out who is pulling the strings, creating the violence. More than likely, there is a connection to the Florida group."

"You don't know that!" snapped Phillips. "One's a socialist group attempting to win over protestors, and the other is an armed and dangerous militia using highly sophisticated weaponry to attack the country. It looks like two separate groups to me. Focus on the militia, the most dangerous of the two."

"Yes, sir," Stein agreed, realizing Director Phillips was quite correct.

"Ask my admin Jacqueline to send you all of the intel we have received thus far on the Florida group. Hopefully that will open up some avenues for you to find them on the Dark Web."

"Yes, sir, but Jacqueline left early today. She is attending the funeral of her brother."

"Jacqueline's brother died? Why, I didn't even know she had a brother."

"Yes, sir. I was told her brother died fairly suddenly."

"I see. Well, get Edna to pull the files, then, and send them to you," requested Stein. He turned and exited the office but stopped before reaching the door. "Oh, and Gary, I'm not dismissing your other lead in Chicago," Phillips added. "You may be right about a link. Dedicate one of your staff to that situation. But please keep the rest of your team here fully focused on Florida. I want leads, good intel, by the end of the day. President Fallon was down there this week and looked quite shaken by what he had seen and heard from the police and relatives of those killed."

Stein returned to his office and called a meeting with his five best tech opp experts. He was determined to get Director Phillips good information that would shed a light on the Florida massacre.

Meanwhile, Dylan had returned to his Monroe Street apartment in Chicago, believing their efforts at Bedford Manor had greatly diminished the threat from the domestic terrorist group. That was a short-lived victory lap, however, when he heard the news about the horrific Florida attack. Watching the news reports, he was seething with anger that anyone could commit such an atrocity. And as a devout Catholic, he was doubly livid that his faith had been the target of the mass murderers.

He quickly checked in with a few of his contacts in Washington, to see if he could learn anything more about that attack. They were working on it, he was told.

Then, he called Father Quilty to find out what the Church leadership was going to do about the situation. Dylan knew the geographical location of the attack wouldn't dispel fear from Catholics anywhere in the country. It wasn't a Florida attack. It was an attack against Catholics. People would rightfully believe that until the killers were caught, all Catholic churches and parishioners were potential targets.

"We have been directed by Cardinal Dillon in New York to have twenty-four-hour security guards added," Father Quilty informed Dylan with a strong note of anxiety in his voice. "And churches are to be closed and locked before and after mass until this situation is resolved and the killers brought to justice."

"Well, Father, I think that is a very good and sound plan right now," Dylan responded, trying to be as encouraging and supportive as possible to his friend. "You have my number, if there is anything I can do."

When Dylan finished his call, he immediately checked the *Chicago Tribune*, where he read a story by columnist John Maas, who was calling for lawful-minded citizens to start standing up to the attacks on the city. Maas believed those attacks had been caused by a socialist group. Dylan had made that same call to action to Chicagoans the previous year in Grant Park.

On that memorable day, Dylan had known he was making a very difficult request. Most citizens weren't physically or mentally prepared, capable or willing to stand up for themselves. Most lived in fear, hoping nothing bad came across their path where they were forced to react, respond, perhaps even fight back.

Dylan tore out the very insightful article from Maas and would keep it to remind others of the realities of the world they lived in. It was a dangerous world. And 2015 was proving to be incredibly dangerous, with both domestic terrorism and violent protests taking place across the country at the same time. It seemed strange, Dylan thought. The country seemed to be getting hit from both the left and the right in unison. He wondered if it was possible there could be some kind of connection.

He sat down to see if there were any updates on the news.

On CSPAN, the anchor was going live to the White House. What came on the screen caught Dylan's full attention as he leaned forward to watch. There was his pal Ken Hack, who had returned to work and was being given a hero's welcome, including a commendation directly from President Fallon. His wife Elizabeth was by his side at the ceremony, which was covered by the White House press corps. It was all smiles that afternoon, Hack mostly happy because his wife had survived the brutal abuse by the cowards who had captured her.

A Q&A session with the press followed, and Elizabeth was asked if there was anything she regretted about that encounter. "Yes," replied Elizabeth with great energy and conviction. "I regret that when I invited those punks to untie me and then try taking a punch at me, they backed down. Because I promise you that I would have kicked the ass of every one of those four cowards."

In a rare show of support, some of the women in the press corps began cheering. The other reporters smiled and joined the applause. Elizabeth Hack was a hero. She was a courageous hero who had been at the brink of death and had remained defiant through it all. In the end, there she stood in the White House, receiving a commendation, while the four bullies lay in the morgue in Washington.

Although Elizabeth was the proud wife of another American hero, she mirrored her husband's patriotic pride and willingness to fight back. They had both been soldiers in the Afghanistan War, which is where they had met. They clicked from day one, seemingly agreeing on anything and everything. They were a great couple. There was nothing opposite about them, but they were entirely attracted to each other, dismissing the oft-stated cliché about why men and women become attracted to each other.

She was well aware that the plan Ken had worked out with Dylan Reilly to save her was very risky. But she knew that if she had been in the same situation, she would have done exactly the same thing. And the beauty of the plan was that it had worked!

Prior to that day, very few people knew Elizabeth or Ken Hack. But following the press conference, the entire country—the entire world—learned about those two great and courageous heroes. They gave Americans hope during a chaotic time in the country, when it was most needed.

"Don't accept these attacks on our country," implored Hack, answering a reporter's question about what regular Americans could do under these violent circumstances. "These may seem like isolated attacks, but I promise you that they are not. This is an orchestrated attack on our country. We all have to stand up to them. They need to know they will be stopped at every corner of our great country."

Having just read Maas' column and hearing Ken echo the same call to action, Dylan thought that perhaps some people might be inspired enough to fight back. He hoped so, for everyone's sake.

Dylan sat in his living room, watching the CSPAN coverage of Ken and Elizabeth speaking to the media. He, too, had been invited to the White House for a commendation but felt it was better to stay anonymous, so the enemy wouldn't know he was involved. He was concerned for his new friends, Ken and Elizabeth, knowing such a public display would make them even bigger targets. But they had already been on the radar of the enemy, so they had nothing to lose and were there to inspire the country to fight back.

Dylan prayed they would be successful.

CHAPTER TWELVE

A hoard of angry millennial protestors descended upon the Columbus statue on Roosevelt Road near Lake Shore Drive in Chicago as the sun was beginning to set over the city's beautiful skyline on a Friday evening in early June.

More than sixty police officers, only a few wearing helmets and riot gear, encircled the famed statue of the Italian explorer, who was credited with discovering the New World, America, in 1492.

Columbus was a major figure of pride for Italian Americans. He was more than just an explorer who had discovered America. He was an adventurous example millions of Italians had followed, traveling across the dangerous Atlantic Ocean with the hope of starting a new life, a better life. His story had motivated Italians from the towns of Verese, in the north, to Ragusa, in the south, to make that long and dangerous journey over waters that had claimed so many lives.

They were encouraged by the opportunity to help build America, which was exactly what millions of proud immigrants from the booted peninsula of Europe had done, creating a better life for themselves and their families.

On the fringe of the very large group of protestors that early evening, stood Marty Mahoney. After witnessing the protest on Fullerton a week earlier, he had seen the Twitter notices, directed to CIU students, about this rally and felt strongly about attending in order to document what was really happening, providing an inside perspective. After viewing how the media had covered the Fullerton protest, most proactively reporting positively about the students' actions, he was going to be sure to document the truth for all of Chicago to see.

When he arrived at the Columbus Drive meeting point in Grant Park, near the softball fields south of Balbo, he blended in by wearing black jeans and holding his black umbrella, as instructed via Twitter. Standing among the sea of students who were only a couple hundred yards away from the statue, the leaders of the group directed them to open up the umbrellas and put on their black shirts. Mahoney, committed to playing the part in order to gain full access, pulled a black t-shirt out of his backpack and quickly put it on. Unlike most of the other protestors, whose shirts read, "BLM" or "Black Lives Matter," Mahoney had chosen a shirt that read "White Sox" in large white letters across the front of it.

After putting on his shirt, out of the corner of his eye, he saw someone quickly approaching him.

"Hey, dude, what's with the White Sox shirt?" asked the dark-haired hipster, Slagle, whom Marty recognized from the CIU signup table and Fullerton protest.

Not skipping a beat, the devoted South Sider responded, "I'm a big Sox fan. And the shirt is black, so it's perfect."

"No, man, it's not! It's not perfect," whined the little goateed organizer.

A few seconds later, Slagle was joined by his tall, balding pal from CIU, Kamus. "Dude, you're supposed to be wearing a BLM shirt," Kamus informed Marty with a highly disappointed look of disgust on his face.

"Sorry. I'll bring one next time," Marty replied with a smile, then tried to change the subject. "Hey, great crowd, huh?"

"Yeah, man. We are going to tear down that statue of American pride tonight," claimed the hipster, pumping his fist in the air.

"I don't think we ever officially met," said Marty, now ready to start documenting the protest by getting the names of the two Abbie Hoffman wannabes from CIU.

"Oh, yeah," agreed the scruffy goateed boy. "I'm Rob Slagle, and this is Tim Kamus. We're, like, die-hard socialists, man. You know what I mean, man?"

"Hey, who isn't, huh?" laughed Mahoney, the joke going right over the heads of dumb and dumber standing in front of him.

"Oh, man, I'm glad to hear that," revealed Kamus, a twenty-year-old Greek American from Rogers Park, who had a reputation in his neighborhood as the biggest pandering suck-up on the North Side. "You know, we have a group that meets every Sunday morning in Wrigleyville, if you want to join us."

"Oh, is that right?" asked Mahoney, realizing he may have tapped into a socialist organization meeting. This was exactly the type of information he had hoped to gain when he had decided to attend the rally. "Why don't you write down the address and time, and I'll be there," requested the first-time undercover agent, who knew this experience would benefit him in his future as a prosecutor.

"Well, why don't we just text it to you, man?" asked Slagle, pulling out his cell phone, preparing to type in the number.

"Honestly, I'm just better with paper, when it comes to addresses, you know," lied Marty, who had no intention of giving out his name or phone number. "If you could just write it down, that would great. Thanks."

Within a few seconds, Kamus had jotted down the information on a protest flyer and handed it to his new redheaded socialist brother-in-arms. "Here you go, dude," shared Kamus. "And we didn't get your name."

"Oh, yeah. It's uh… It's Joe Jackson," lied Marty again, using the name of the great White Sox left fielder from days long gone. He knew they would have no clue about Shoeless Joe.

To seal the new fake friendship, Marty fist bumped and half-hugged with the Beavis and Butthead of American protestors, which he knew was their standard way of greeting or parting with their leftist supporters.

Just then, a Hispanic student approached them. Marty immediately recognized him as one of the protest leaders at the Fullerton rally. "Hey, quit the chitchat, man! We've got to get this rally moving before that sun sets," he informed his two compatriots, then looked at Marty. "Who is this guy?"

"Oh, hey, Darius. This Joe Jackson," said Kamus, exhibiting his ignorance about one of the most famous names in baseball.

A curious look crossed the face of Darius Ramirez, which made Marty nervous. Was this guy a real baseball fan? "Joe Jackson?" he questioned, looking somewhat skeptical about the name. "Wasn't there a famous soccer player named Joe Jackson?"

Before Marty could respond, Ramirez corrected himself. "No, no. Not soccer. Baseball."

Marty felt the blood rush to his head. He wondered if he had made a terrible mistake. Would they ask to see his license, he wondered. If they did, he decided that he would just take off and run like he was out to set a new cross-country record. He was sure as hell not going to give up his identity to these three Bozos.

"Yeah, Joe Jackson. Baseball. That's it!" Darius corrected himself again, as Marty prepared to run. "Oh, wait. I'm thinking of Bo Jackson."

"Bo Jackson!" Marty exclaimed with delight, now feeling extremely relieved that the recall of the baseball historian in front of him only went as far back as the 1980s. "Yeah, Bo Jackson. He was great! He played for the White Sox!"

"Right," agreed Darius, giving Marty a dirty look. "Bring a BLM shirt next time, man." Ramirez began looking around as if he had lost something, or someone. "Hey, where's Ron?" he asked his two compatriots.

"He's got lookout duty," informed Kamus, watching Ramirez nod his approval. "Jeffrey wants to be sure we spot Reilly in case he shows up."

"Yeah, that's smart," agreed Ramirez. "Well, let's go!"

Marty watched Ramirez, Slagle and Kamus walk to the front of the pack. Evidently, they would be leading this rally as well. Darius, who no question was the brightest of the three socialist dipshits, loudly directed approximately fifteen hundred protestors to walk south down Columbus Drive toward the Christopher Columbus statue.

It only took five minutes to reach the memorial, which sat on a large, round four-stepped cement pedestal in Grant Park, about twenty-five yards east of Columbus Drive, just north of Roosevelt Road. About a dozen uniformed police officers stood in front of the statue and had access to the pedestal blocked off by blue wooden barricades.

Seeing the barricades and police presence, Ramirez quickly turned to the crowd and began chanting, "Columbus Must Go! Columbus Must Go!"

The mob followed his lead, chanting in unison, trying to muster up as much false anger as their non-existent acting skills would allow.

The red-haired southwest sider stayed on the outside of the pack, where he knew he could make a quick getaway, if needed. He most certainly didn't join in on the chants and derogatory slurs, which he could see was gaining the attention of a few of the protestors in front of him. One grungy, full-bearded student turned and gave him an angry look, like he was staring at a traitor.

Quickly thinking, Marty raised his hands and began using sign language. The bearded fellow just nodded and gave him the thumbs-up sign to apologize, because he was obviously a very nice and thoughtful fellow. Then, he went back to chanting, "Police suck! Down with America!"

Marty had a bird's-eye view of the police surrounding the statue. Only a few were wearing full police riot gear, while most were dressed only in their uniforms, bright blue shirts with navy slacks and black boots.

Mahoney spotted a few of the fellows from his neighborhood who had just graduated from the Chicago Police Academy. Even though he was there as an undercover investigator, hoping to provide the authorities with good inside intelligence, he almost felt guilty about standing with the protestors.

What if one of his neighborhood cops saw him standing there? If that happened, he decided he would take the dirty looks and just straighten it out later with them. He moved a few steps into the crowd, hoping to avoid that moment of visual derision.

As Ramirez continued leading the chants and marched the group right up to the barricades, Marty watched Kamus and Slagle take off their black backpacks. They unzipped their polyester bags and started giving instructions to some of the protestors around them. Then, they dumped out frozen water bottles and rocks.

Within seconds, protestors began hurling the potentially lethal objects at the police, who worked to dodge them. It looked like a game of dodgeball, except this was no game. Some of the cops were hit by the rocks and bottles and fell backwards onto the cement, badly injured.

Some were hit the head. A few in the chest. One in the face. This was now a battle, a war. And Marty was standing on the wrong side of the battle line. He grew angry, wishing to fight back against the group of misguided bottle- and rock-throwers. He glared at Slagle, Kamus and Ramirez, who were orchestrating the attack.

The police had been asked to be non-violent, yet they were facing an angry, violent mob. Then, someone threw a lit M-80 fire-bomb, which exploded directly in front of one of the lady cops. The twenty-something-year-old police officer screamed as it exploded. It tore into her leg, and she fell to the ground in tremendous pain.

The protestors cheered.

Captain Phil Parlick was in charge of the detail. He had become famous the year before for spotting the hotel shooter who had been spraying bullets across MusicFest in Grant Park, killing dozens of innocent people, including Dylan's wife. Thanks to Captain Parlick, a police sniper had shot and killed Peter Stephens, who had been positioned with his assault rifle in the window of a twentieth-floor Michigan Avenue hotel room, ending his reign of terror.

Now Parlick found himself in the same park but dealing with a different crisis. Seeing his injured officer down, he quickly called in the paramedics. The veteran officer had seen enough of this attack and ordered his officers to stop the riot. Armed with billy clubs and Glock guns at the ready, the police advanced toward the rock-throwing protestors. Three cops swung their clubs, beating back the protestors, while the chants got louder and meaner: "Fuck you, pigs! Fuck you, pigs!"

This was the shot that led off all five newscasts that evening. Once again, it made the police look like the bad guys, when they were only retaliating and defending themselves against a vicious attack upon them.

It was reminiscent of the 1968 Democratic Convention riots outside the Hilton Hotel, when hippies with razor blades in their shoes had kicked the cops in the shins. The news cameras had missed that shot. They had also missed the yippies filling baggies full of urine and feces and throwing them at the police officers.

And when the cops had retaliated with billy clubs, that visual became the lead story on each news broadcast. That visual became the misrepresented history of that protest, which continued to the present day, in documentaries and news retrospectives.

In front of the Columbus Statue on that day, Marty could see the fight twenty yards in front of him. The redhead's face filled with anger. He looked around at all of the protestors who were caught up in the moment, caught up in the hysteria being created by the three socialist troublemakers at the front of the crowd.

Out of the corner of his eye, Marty then saw a thirty-something-year-old, brown-bearded man standing behind a tall, thick elm tree about forty yards from the statue, on the east side, near Roosevelt Road. The man was wearing a tan camouflage military coat and cap. It was a hot night. Marty knew something wasn't right. No one would be wearing a coat in the hot weather, unless they were concealing something. He wondered if the man was there to retaliate against the protestors.

That was when the man turned in Marty's direction, and he could see it was Longhair, the leader of the Fullerton protest, a week earlier. Seeing the now-infamous Chester Walling, adrenaline shot through Marty's entire body. He was certain something was going to happen. Something bad!

Longhair had his long locks tucked under the military cap, but Marty knew his face. No doubt in his mind it was Chester Walling, the instigator of the Fullerton protest. This was the same man who had confused the CBS reporter. He was the same man who was intent on spewing messages about bringing down America.

Marty didn't know what to do. Should he run up to the cops and let them know, he wondered. That seemed like the right thing to do. He took off running around the perimeter of the crowd, craning his neck over the protestors to keep an eye on Longhair. That was when he saw the socialist leader pull out an AK-15 assault rifle.

Oh, no, thought Marty!

Another adrenaline rush! Mahoney sprinted faster, looking over the crowd at the man, who was now pointing the assault rifle at the cops. Oh, no! He had to get the police before Walling fired. He was still too far away. Longhair was going to kill the police.

Then, all of a sudden, Marty saw the gun fly forward, out of the shooter's hand. Walling quickly bent over in pain, grabbing his right hand. He started looking around, saw something and began running east toward Lake Shore Drive.

Marty stopped. He was almost at the front of the crowd, near the statue. He started running toward Walling to see what was happening. And that was when he first saw him, Dylan Reilly. The Dylan Reilly! He was sprinting like The Flash after the shooter.

Everyone knew he was the fastest gun, but he was also fast afoot. Real fast! As a track star, Marty could certainly appreciate someone with that kind of speed. Dylan sprinted down Roosevelt Road and drew closer to Longhair. Marty took off running after them, hoping to see it all.

Longhair sprinted across an open Lake Shore Drive with Reilly forty yards behind him. As Longhair reached the lakefront, he must have realized there was nowhere to hide. Then, the tan-jacketed socialist stopped and quickly pulled out a Glock gun from his right jacket pocket, turned, and aimed at Dylan. Not quick enough.

While still in full stride, Reilly pulled out his famed six-shooter and, with lightning-fast speed, shot Longhair twice in the chest. The tan-jacketed shooter flew backwards onto the cement pavement along the lake. His cap flew off his head. His long mane tumbled out. The Glock gun hit the cement pavement at the same time as Walling, who bounced hard twice before resting still.

Blood trickled from his chest. His hair now covered half of his face. The high waves from Lake Michigan crashed against the cement barrier, sending a shower of water across the dead socialist, washing the dark blood off the front of his tan jacket.

Marty stood on the west side of Lake Shore Drive watching the incredible scene. His eyes wide and jaw dropped, the redheaded college freshman saw Reilly approach the prone man. He bent over and checked his pulse. A wave crashed behind him, sprinkling lake water across Dylan's wavy brown hair, white collared shirt, blue jean pants and brown chukka boots. The half-drenched hero stood and stepped away from Lake Michigan's powerful water display in order to make a call on his cell phone.

Police Captain Parlick took the call and quickly dispatched two of his officers and a paddy wagon to pick up the attacker.

Marty could not take his eyes off of Reilly. A year earlier, he had watched the news reports about him, but seeing him up close was absolutely amazing. Exhilarating! He hadn't flinched. He wasn't afraid. And he was so fast!

A spine-tingling sensation shot up the redhead's spine, like he had just witnessed a superhero action movie. Only this was no movie. It was real! A smile grew on his face. He was so happy he had witnessed that moment. He knew Reilly had saved those cops protecting the statue.

None of the protestors or media covering the rally seemed to be aware of what had just happened only a couple hundred yards away. They were all focused on the Columbus statue and the protestors. They had all missed the main event. They had missed what could have been the biggest story in the country that evening, had anyone besides the redheaded college kid seen it.

Mahoney continued watching as two police officers, who had been dispatched to the scene of the shooting, jogged up to the man many called The Fastest Gun. They stayed with the prone attacker, while Dylan Reilly ran quickly back across Lake Shore Drive and toward the statue.

Mahoney just stood and watched Dylan run past him. He wanted to say something, but didn't, couldn't.

When Reilly arrived at the statue, he stepped front and center on the cement platform alongside Chicago's finest, who by this time, had brought some semblance of order to the riot. As he shook hands with Captain Parlick, the protestors stopped their chanting, knowing immediately who they were looking at. They recognized the good-looking man with brown wavy hair, and soaked white shirt, blue jeans and boots. It was America's hero. He had their attention. The police captain handed him the megaphone.

"This is supposed to be a peaceful protest," announced Dylan, looking behind him to see several of the officers lying on the ground, injured, with paramedics attending to them.

"Black Lives Matter!" shouted one of the protestors, a black teen who was a member of the BLM organization.

"Yes, black lives do matter," announced Reilly with great vigor, looking back once again. "And I'm looking at four black police officers lying on the ground. Bleeding! Badly injured! You did that!"

"They're cops, man! They're cops!" shouted Kamus, looking around, waving to the protestors, trying to incite their anger.

"So black cops' lives don't matter? Is that what you're saying?"

"They're pigs, man! Pigs!" yelled Slagle, still holding a frozen water bottle.

"Yeah, pigs!" Ramirez chanted, pumping his fist in the air.

A chorus of boos followed, aimed at the three detractors, the three leaders of the protest. The crowd had turned on them.

"All black lives matter," bellowed a young lady with pink and purple hair, holding up her BLM sign. "All lives matter!"

Most in the crowd cheered the colorful, courageous lady, while others continued booing the three troublemakers. Some of the students moved in on them, pushing them, shouting in their faces.

Ramirez, Kamus and Slagle could readily see that the tide had turned against them and it was time to go. They walked quickly away, toward Columbus Drive. But five teenage boys followed them. They ran. The teens ran. The race was on.

The TV crews captured all of it and would be showing it later on their news broadcasts.

Dylan watched their escape and smiled. The crowd had come to their senses. The police captain nudged one of his officers to follow the three radicals.

The TV crews turned their cameras back toward Reilly.

"Some of you may know, I taught history in high school," Dylan revealed to the now calmer and more rational group of young students. "And I'm telling you, this effort to tear down statues of Columbus, Washington, Jefferson… It's misguided. And with all due respect, it only shows that you need to go back and study the history of this country one more time."

Some started booing him at that proclamation.

"Hey, man! Don't boo him!" ordered a tough, athletic-looking young man. "That's Dylan Reilly!"

Silence. Calm.

"Thank you!" expressed Dylan to the young man. Then, he addressed the protestors again. "Some of you aren't willing to accept the times that those historical figures lived in. You're trying to apply your mindset from today's social norms to those times. It wasn't 2015. It was 1492, in this case. It was 1776, for the other two great Americans. The times were different. There was a lot of brutality, a lot of violence. Attitudes were different. Beliefs were different. If you want to be honest, you should be able to respect them for what they did during the times they lived in."

"Fuck you, Reilly!" yelled a dirty, long-haired young man in the front row, hurling a frozen bottle at him.

Boom! The bottle exploded in mid-air, easy target practice for Dylan, who had pulled his six-shooter out with lightning-fast speed.

Silence. Thousands of wide eyes starred at The Fastest Gun.

Most stood stunned, actually having seen just how fast Dylan could draw a gun and shoot so accurately. Protestors who a moment ago had hateful, wild eyes, now had fear in their eyes.

"Are you going to shoot us?" a girl yelled out, looking truly frightened for her life. "Please don't shoot us!"

"No, young lady, I'm not going to shoot you," he informed her. "I stop bad guys. I stop people trying to do harm to innocent people. A few minutes ago, you weren't protesting peacefully. You were obviously being misled by three young radicals with bad intentions, who are currently being chased across Grant Park.

"Now, I know you all have good intentions, or you wouldn't be here today. I strongly recommend you all go back home now and reconsider what you are doing, how you are doing it, and who is influencing you."

As Dylan was addressing the crown, the three radicals sprinting across the softball fields in Grant Park had been caught by the group of teenage boys and were paying for their actions.

"Those three men that left here are most likely part of a socialist activist group trying to destroy our country," Dylan continued. "Is that what you want?"

"No! We love America, but we want racism to end!" yelled out Pink and Purple.

"I know you do," Dylan confirmed, scanning the faces in front of him, which were now focused on his every word. "But you're being misled. There is at least one group, maybe two, trying to take advantage of this movement and use you for their own purposes."

"That's total BS!" yelled a man in the crowd, whom Dylan couldn't see among the mass of young faces. Captain Parlick talked into his walkie-talkie, dispatching a young, black plainclothes officer to weave into the crowd to see if she could identify him.

"Just a few minutes ago, there was a man with an assault rifle right over there, near that thick elm tree," said Dylan, pointing toward the tree near Roosevelt Road. "He was just about to shoot all of these police officers up here. These are the men and women committed to keeping this city safe, to keeping you safe. Is that what you want?"

Silence. The news of the shooter sent a shock wave through the crowd as well as the TV news reporters, who realized they had just missed a major story.

Most of the young people had entered the park that night thinking they could protest and not have to worry about anyone actually getting hurt. Now they had seen several police officers injured right in front of them. And then, they had learned about a man with a gun. This wasn't what they had signed up for at CIU. This wasn't "RESIST." It was "ATTACK!"

"We want the police to stop shooting innocent black people!" yelled a young black man wearing a BLM cap.

"I do, too! So do they!" pronounced Dylan, watching the plainclothes officer thread her way to the middle of the pack. "But you shouldn't lose sight of the fact that they are also the ones protecting all of you. You take them out of the equation, and it's anarchy. Pure anarchy!"

"Anarchy! Yeah! Bring down this capitalist country!" yelled that same angry male voice. The young plainclothes officer spotted the man, and within seconds, she was leading him out of the crowd toward a paddy wagon for questioning. The crowd around her cheered as she marched him out.

Marty could now see him. It was Mr. Bulging Eyes. Obviously, this was the man Ramirez had asked about earlier, the lookout responsible for alerting them if Dylan Reilly showed up at the rally.

Well, despite his huge eyes, he had obviously missed Reilly entering the area, thankfully.

"I know most of you mean well," admitted Dylan, nodding at the captain, signaling a great job apprehending the angry protestor. "That's why you are out here. But that group is taking advantage of your protests to try and bring down America! They may be associated with the same group that attacked the White House. They may be the same group that massacred those innocent men, women and children in the church in Florida. I know none of you—not one of you—stands behind those actions!"

"I do!" yelled out Mr. Bulging Eyes, one last rant before he was firmly guided into the paddy wagon by the lady cop. A loud chorus of boos arose, aimed directly at him, letting him know he had no support.

"No, we don't stand behind those actions!" yelled Pink and Purple, who had now taken the position as spokesperson for the protestors. "How do you know all of this?"

"Because we captured a few of them and found out directly from the source," Dylan informed them. "It's happening. And all of you need to ask yourselves which side you stand on—America or these socialists trying to tear our country apart."

"America, man! America!" yelled out a large number of the protestors in unison.

The chant began: "America! America!"

The police captain smiled. The injured police officers on the ground could hear it clearly and looked relieved. A few of the injured cops were able to make it back up to their feet. A loud cheer rose for the now-standing officers. The tide had turned. Sensibility and patriotism had arrived, thanks to the rational appeal of Dylan Reilly.

As the protestors began leaving, Marty Mahoney realized that most of them had come with one mindset and were leaving with a completely different attitude and perspective about who was the real threat in America.

Later, the news reported that the man with the rifle, whom Reilly had shot, was indeed Chester Walling, a known socialist radical with a long arrest and prison record. Walling claimed to have been a decorated Vietnam veteran, but police revealed he had been a cook in the army for a year, before he had been thrown out for being a pathological liar and a danger to his unit.

Reports also confirmed Dylan Reilly's speculation about Kamus, Slagle and Ramirez. They had been arrested and proudly admitted to being part of a socialist group. They claimed, however, that they weren't responsible for the frozen bottles and rocks thrown at the police. The news footage showed students throwing the rocks and bottles, but not one station had caught the three radicals in the act. So unfortunately, the police didn't have enough to hold them, and they were released.

Marty knew better. He had seen it all for himself. He sat on his brown leather couch in the family room of his home in Mt. Greenwood and picked up the BLM flyer with the information about the socialists' meeting on Sunday. He would get the evidence the cops needed.

CHAPTER THIRTEEN

Marty Mahoney stood still for a minute, maybe two, staring at the front door of the greystone three-story home in Wrigleyville on this sunny Sunday morning. This was the North Side of Chicago, an area of the city he would never normally venture into very often.

He glanced at his silver watch. It was 10 o'clock sharp, right on time.

This was no small decision. If he walked up those eight weather-beaten cement steps and through that tall oak front door, he knew it would be a risk. How big a risk was the question. He didn't know.

Determined to succeed with his personal investigation of the group, he gritted his teeth, opened the black metal gate and quickly walked up the eight stairs. He knocked three times on the brown-stained door.

"He's here!" Mahoney could hear a voice say from behind the door, which was opened by a familiar face, that of Robert Slagle.

When Marty walked in the door, he was fairly nervous about how he would be received. But at the same time, he was determined to bring down these three radicals and hopefully find out enough information that could really help the police.

A few minutes later, he was seated at an old oak table in the dining room. Mahoney purposely sat in the hardwood chair placed in the right corner of the table, closest to the front door, in the event he had to make a quick exit. Next to him sat Darius Ramirez. Directly across the table sat Slagle, with Tim Kamus on his right.

Marty had mentally prepared himself for every tough question he thought they might ask him upon his arrival.

"So what happened to you on Friday?" asked Slagle, who was wearing a pink shirt, green skinny jeans and bright red boots to accentuate his hipster look.

"I was in the crowd, but you were all up front, so you probably couldn't see me," Marty explained.

"You should have come up there with us, man," said Darius. "You're one of us now. So you've got to step to the front. I'll blame myself for this one, but we could have used you on Friday. Those five punks caught up to us and beat the hell out of us. If we had you, or Ron, I think we could have taken them."

"Yeah, you're right, Darius!" agreed Kamus, who had proven to his other two socialist pals that he was the worst fighter of the three, completely unable to throw a decent punch. The fairly tall Greek American had an average build, but no muscles apparent on his scrawny arms, exposed by the green army t-shirt he was wearing. Marty would have guessed that the out-of-shape, goateed Slagle wasn't much help during the fight, either. It was obvious that Ramirez was the only one of the three who could have put up any kind of battle. He was the most physically fit of the group and looked like an athlete.

Marty couldn't help but think that Kamus and Slagle were the kinds of kids who had been outcasts at school, kids who would never fit in. Darius must have recognized that and recruited them into this North Side socialist chapter, knowing they were probably eager to be invited into any group on campus.

But Marty wondered how Darius had gotten pulled into this group. He was good-looking, smart, confident and athletic. What had motivated him to turn on America?

There was no time to ponder that thought as a tall, thin, balding, brown-haired, long-bearded, thirty-year-old, dressed in a faded green military jacket over a grey t-shirt and worn-out black jeans, stormed into the room with rage in his eyes. Marty immediately speculated that he must be the leader, because he was most certainly older than the others.

"Who the hell is this?" barked Wooten, looking directly at Marty.

"He was with us at the protest," explained Darius, trying to calm their leader down. "We know him from school and the protests. He's good. He can be trusted."

"Really?" Wooten questioned, looking over at Slagle and Kamus. "You two agree?"

"Yes!" they agreed in unison, then looked at each other, both choosing not to say "jinx" during such a heated moment.

"He's at all the protests. He's an ardent socialist, reads Lenin, so he's definitely with us!" informed Slagle, now creating fiction to support the decision to bring Marty to the greystone.

"What's your name, man? Where are you from? Why are you here?"

Marty felt the blood rush to his head as everyone's attention was now on him. "Joe. Joe Jackson. I'm a student at CIU. I joined the protests this month. I'm from Chicago, the Bridgeport neighborhood," Mahoney lied, knowing he couldn't give them any accurate information, or they would come after his family.

"Bridgeport?" Wooten blurted his disappointment.

"Yes, 35th and Shields…"

"A South Sider? You brought a South Sider into this?" screamed Wooten, completely missing the significance of the address Mahoney had just provided him.

"Yes, what's wrong with that?" Darius asked.

"They can't be trusted!" hollered Wooten at the top of his lungs. "That neighborhood is filled with cops and city workers. He may be a police plant, for all I know."

"Sir, if you would like me to leave, I can just go now…"

"No, no, you're in it now, kid, whether you like it or not," Wooten informed him, which sounded more like a death sentence. "As your new friends here can attest, there's only one way out of this organization, and it's not walking out the door. And believe me, if you're a plant, I'll find out. So you had better be an ardent socialist, or this isn't going to end well for you. That I can promise."

Somehow, as threatening as that statement sounded, it didn't bother Marty. No one in the room knew his identity. He already had enough information to pass along to the police to arrest all four of the conspirators. He watched Wooten pace back and forth, his black leather boots clicking against the grey tiled floor with each step.

Marty was just hoping Wooten would say, or do, something to add even more damaging information to his report. After the police had released The Three Commiegos and their bulging-eyed buddy Friday evening, Marty wanted to bring them solid facts about the activities and intent of their socialist organization, to put them behind bars.

"Where is Clapp?" Wooten asked.

"He's on the early shift at Sears today," revealed Darius. "But he'll be here."

"Oh, is that right?" Wooten responded in an ominous tone. "Well, I'm going to have to make it clear to him how important it is to be here on time, to make the full commitment."

Wooten then typed a note into his phone. All watched. Was he keeping a running report card on each of them? Apparently he was.

"Which brings me to the reason I decided to join your Sunday morning meeting today," Wooten began, then bent over, placing his hands on the table, leaning forward to look at his young and inexperienced red army. "What the hell happened at the protest? How did you not spot Reilly earlier?"

"I didn't see him," Kamus chimed in first, quickly trying to deflect any blame. "We were focused on attacking the cops and getting the protestors to join us."

"I didn't, either," admitted Slagle, raising the palms of his hands, signaling he was blameless. "I was helping Tim."

"Darius, who was the lookout?" Wooten demanded, an intense and angry look across his now reddened face. "Who was supposed to be watching the entire area in case something like this happened?"

"I'm sorry, Jeffrey, I don't want to start pointing fingers," deflected Darius.

"Who? Who was the lookout?"

Silence.

With no one willing to take the blame, Wooten reached his right hand into the large pocket of his military jacket and pulled out a .357 Magnum. "Someone had better start talking," Wooten pronounced, checking the cartridge of his very large silver gun, which some referred to as a hand canon.

Silence.

Marty watched the Three Commiegos stare at each other, waiting for the guilty lookout to admit his error, so Wooten wouldn't shoot all of them.

Silence. Then, the front door opened, and in walked Ron Clapp, who had not been expecting to see Wooten standing in front of the table holding a dangerous firearm.

"What do you think this is?" Wooten screamed at the bulging-eyed twenty-three-year-old.

"I'm sorry, Jeffrey!" Clapp begged, hoping not to get shot for coming late. "I took the shift thinking I could get here in time, with the lighter Sunday morning traffic on the Kennedy. There was an accident at Harlem that delayed me. I apologize."

"Fine! Just sit down," Wooten ordered Clapp, who was dressed in a white collared shirt, khaki pants and brown shoes, his basic uniform at work.

Clapp grabbed a stool from the counter and parked it at the front of the table. "I'm sorry, fellows," he apologized to the group. "What did I miss?"

"I'll tell you what you missed," Wooten began, visibly upset. "We were just going over the assignments at the protest the other day. And who was the lookout in case Dylan Reilly showed up?"

"Oh, that was me." Clapp raised his hand, completely

unaware of how angry Wooten was about the botched assignment. "I was watching. I just didn't see him. I saw Chester Walling behind the cement pillar, with his rifle, ready to shoot. And the next time I looked over, he was gone. I looked around but couldn't find him."

"Well, that's because he was running away from Reilly, dipshit! You should have seen that. You should have helped him, and he might be sitting here with us today. And mister hero would be dead, and not Chester!"

"Yes, I know," agreed Clapp, who had actually been distracted by a hipster who had been shoved into him, apologized, but then quickly complimented him on his goatee, which resulted in a quick discussion about goatees and skinny jeans, favorite hipster subjects. "It won't happen again. I promise!"

"Oh, I know it won't," confirmed Wooten. "And all of you at this table had better understand something. As Mr. Medov made clear, there are no second chances here. You get it right the first time. Cause that's the only chance you're going to get from me. Are we clear?"

Marty watched a concerned look grow on Clapp's face. He wasn't aware of the brutal punishment that had taken place in that same room a few weeks earlier, when Wooten's best friend Fontane had been mercilessly murdered by Medov.

Clapp seemed to know exactly what Wooten meant. He looked at Wooten like he was trying to read his eyes. They narrowed. Everyone around the table seemed to notice.

Silence filled the room.

Clapp shot up quickly from his stool and pushed Wooten hard, knocking him backwards to the floor. Then, he darted as fast as he could toward the front door. It was only fifteen feet away.

Marty could see the panic and desperation in Clapp as he ran as fast as he could for the large oak front door. He grabbed the brass doorknob and started to turn it. It looked like he was going to make it out of there.

Wooten recovered quickly and jumped back up on his feet. He ran toward the hallway.

As Clapp pulled the door open and began to exit, the sound of gunshots echoed through the room. Blam! Blam!

Two bullets in the back of the head, just like Medov had done earlier to Fontane. The same spot. The same result. Clapp slumped forward to the floor. Blood splattered all over the door, and red smeared white wall. A puddle of red formed on the gray tile.

Mahoney's eyes grew wide, his jaw dropped, his heart raced. He now knew for certain the risk he had undertaken to accomplish his mission. He looked across the table at Kamus, who looked scared to death.

"Slagle, Kamus, pick him up and put him in my trunk!" Wooten ordered. "You, too, Darius! And let this be a lesson to each of you. You don't make mistakes."

"Don't worry, Jeffrey," said Kamus, keeping his world-class kiss-ass reputation intact. "We won't. We get it."

"Get his body out of here. And one of you keep watch to make sure no one sees you doing it. Understand?"

Not one of the three volunteered to keep watch, given what had just happened to Clapp.

"Okay, Red, you're on watch."

"Yes, sir. I will," Marty confirmed, just hoping for the moment when he could get away from this group of terrorists and go to the cops.

"'Yes, sir.' I like that," announced Wooten, a smile now growing on his face as he looked at the other three. "I want all of you calling me 'sir' from now on. I'm the general of this terrorist group. Salute me, too, from now on. We may be socialists, but we are a red army as well. So that's the way it's going to be. Got it?"

"Yes, sir," all three bellowed out at the same time, saluting Wooten, hoping not to get shot. Then, they moved quickly over to Clapp's bloody body. Within minutes, Kamus and Ramirez had him stuffed into the trunk of Wooten's red 2010 Lada Riva.

When they returned, Wooten pulled Ramirez aside and instructed him to get all of Marty's information. Like with everyone else, once Wooten had his personal information, he could get him to do anything he needed. If Marty were to try and leave the organization, Wooten would go after his family.

"And clean up that mess in there, too!" he ordered them, driving off in a huff.

For the next ten minutes, Ramirez and Kamus attempted to get Marty's personal information, while Slagle cleaned up the bloody mess at the front door.

"I left my wallet and cell phone at home," Marty explained to them. "I thought in case the cops raided the place, it would be best not to have any identification on me.

Ramirez was no dummy and didn't trust that explanation. He frisked Marty head to toe. Nothing. Marty was telling the truth. Well, at least they thought so. As an experienced chess player, Marty always liked to stay two moves ahead of his opponent and had hidden his phone and wallet in a bush a block away, prior to entering the house that morning.

Ramirez asked him write down his address, phone number and email address.

The redhead undercover investigator agreed, writing down his address, 333 W. 35th Street, Chicago, Illinois, which was the address to the White Sox ballpark.

"Oh, yeah, that's definitely in Bridgeport," blurted Kamus, trying to appear knowledgeable about the city and its neighborhoods."

"What about social media—your Twitter handle, Facebook, Instagram? You must have those," questioned Ramirez, still hoping to get some solid information.

"I'm sorry to say it, but my parents made me get off of social media last year, when there was a big fight at school that was started by two students getting into a pissing match about politics on Twitter," Marty informed them, hoping he would be alive to see a confessional at church in the next few days.

"Okay, but text me the second you get home, understand?" barked Ramirez, who had to know that sending Marty out the door without his personal information was very risky.

"And I'll scan in my license and email it to you this afternoon," Marty lied. "If you can all just write down your email addresses here."

Without blinking an eye, Kamus not only wrote down his email addresses, but added his full name and phone number. Ramirez wasn't that stupid.

"Just use Tim's. I'll send you mine later, after you text me," he allowed, opening the front door for Marty. "The second you get home, text Tim."

"Will do," agreed Marty, feeling so happy to be out of the horrific situation. As he walked toward the Addison Avenue el station, he stopped at the bush, where he found his wallet and cell phone hidden under the leaves, just as he had left them. He smiled. He felt such relief.

Only ten minutes later, Mahoney boarded the Red Line headed toward the Loop. He felt like he had escaped death and would never put himself in that risky position again. Exiting at Harrison Street, Marty flew up the stairs from the subway station and sprinted the two blocks to the LaSalle Street Metra Train Station. Up the escalator he ran and around the corridor to the 2:10 Rock Island train, which was just about to leave.

"Wait!" yelled the barely winded cross-country star, getting the attention of the conductor, who held the doors open until the redheaded flash flew up onto the steps of the shiny silver train. He maneuvered his way up the staircase to the second deck, plopping down in the first tan-colored seat, which had another seat across from it. Up went his feet. Ah! He was comfortable and happy. Safe!

He couldn't wait to get to his stop at 107th Street in Beverly. In his mind, he was already calculating how quickly he would be able to run home from the station.

As the train passed White Sox Park, he checked his phone for any news on the terrorists. There were no updates. He checked Twitter. Just a lot of protestors ranting about being misled by the socialist leaders at the Columbus statue.

All Marty knew for certain was the second he walked in the door of his lifelong South Millard Street home, he was definitely going to contact the Chicago Police. He would have to talk with his parents as well, so they were well aware of the situation. This wasn't the time to assume that nothing would ever come back at him. It was a dangerous game he was playing. He had to cover all of his bases.

For a brief second, he had considered going to one of his neighbors, all of whom were veteran police officers. But he realized going straight to the chief was the right decision, given the important information he would share. And he most definitely wanted to get it all off of his chest and conscience as quickly as possible.

Looking out the window at the passing landscape, the Metra train couldn't move fast enough for him to get home on this sunny Sunday afternoon in June.

CHAPTER FOURTEEN

Wearing a White Sox cap and black hoodie sweatshirt on this unusually cool and windy Wednesday morning in June, Marty Mahoney stood on the west side of Buckingham Fountain, scanning the area. He was nervous. Very nervous! He hadn't been able to sleep well since he had left the terrorists' Wrigleyville home three days earlier.

There were quite a few people walking through Grant Park. Many stopped at the metal fence forming the perimeter around the famous fountain. Paranoid, Mahoney thought they were all eyeballing him, even though most looked more like tourists, instead of terrorists.

Holding his hat tightly on his head so it wouldn't be blown away by the strong wind coming off the lake, he stared intently back and forth across the area. He couldn't shake his anxiety. He knew this would be his state of mind until Wooten was arrested and jailed. Marty knew that once Wooten realized he wasn't coming back and could expose the terror group, it would place Slagle, Kamus and Ramirez in jeopardy. He most certainly didn't support their actions, but he didn't want to see them get two bullets to the back of the head like Clapp. Now he was going to find out if his decision to go to the police would help, stopping Wooten before he could do any further harm.

As he stood there, he saw a Middle Eastern-looking man in a black cotton hoodie and matching pants running toward him. Mahoney looked around quickly, trying to determine if he should run. The man got closer. He could feel his face flush, and he started to sweat. Just before he was ready to run, the man veered off to his right and yelled out, "Barkley! Barkley!"

Marty looked over to see a small white Bichon running toward the hedges. The man had lost his dog for a moment.

Young Mahoney put his hand over his face and started talking to himself. "Calm down! Calm down! No one knows you're here. They don't know your name!"

"Marty Mahoney." A voice rang out in front of him. Adrenaline shot through his entire body. Wide-eyed and dry-mouthed, he looked up to see a smiling police officer who was quite familiar to him.

Captain Gregory Panozzo had become familiar to him and all of America since the Midwest Trade Building attacks a year earlier.

Marty took a deep breath. He could feel his heart racing, but suddenly was completely relieved.

"Mr. Mahoney?" The friendly Italian American officer approached him, reaching out to shake hands with the young man, who was now visibly shaking a bit. "Hey, no need to be nervous. I'm here to help."

Marty had chosen this meeting place instead of the police station, believing that Wooten might have people watching police headquarters, looking for him.

"I know," nodded Marty, starting to walk south toward the hedges, where he thought they would have a little more privacy. "This is all very dangerous, something I never expected to be involved in. They're killers, Captain Panozzo! I saw it!"

Panozzo put his left hand on the young man's shoulder, trying to settle him down. Mahoney could see two Chicago Police squad cars parked on Columbus, the police officers inside keeping watch in the event anything went wrong.

"So what exactly happened?" asked the highly decorated policeman as they passed the bench and were now in the hedgerow section, hidden from most who might be walking through the area. Marty described everything that had happened to him. He shared every detail he could remember, beginning with the signup table at CIU and all the protests he had attended. He told Captain Panozzo how he had been at the Columbus statue that Monday night and had seen Dylan Reilly chase down the shooter. He then went on to explain the horrific scene at the greystone in Wrigleyville.

"It's a guy named Jeffrey Wooten!" revealed Mahoney. "He's the one running everything. He shot one of the students in cold blood, and I thought for sure I was next. I was really lucky to get out of there alive."

"Okay, look. You did the right thing," explained Captain Panozzo, looking Marty in the eye, trying to resurrect his confidence. "And I'm sure you're right about Wooten being in charge here, but he's not the one heading up all of this. It goes much further up the chain."

Marty gave him a puzzled look. "Is there really a socialist plot to bring down America?"

"It certainly looks like it," admitted the fifteen-year police veteran. "And they are using these protests to achieve their objective. They have to be stopped."

Marty nodded and started to feel safe for the first time since he had entered Wrigleyville.

"And don't worry about those three other fellows. We'll get them out of there as well."

"Thank you. I'm sure they're not bad guys, just confused."

"Yeah, well, there's a lot of that going around right now."

Captain Panozzo walked Marty over to one of the squad cars and introduced him to his partner, Officer Bob Wingo, a thirty-something black police officer, who had joined the force after playing ten years at second base for the Triple A Charlotte Knights in the minor leagues.

"Marty, this is Officer Wingo, a man I trust with my life," said Panozzo, smiling at his friend. "He'll take you into police headquarters. They'll make sure you and your family are safe. You were smart not to give them your real name."

"Bob, tell the chief that Marty gave me some essential information that will really help us. We will need to meet with the FBI, too. We need to game-plan this."

CHAPTER FIFTEEN

Medov entered the large, richly decorated, but dimly lit, office with much trepidation. His efforts had been severely scrutinized for months, and he knew what his bosses were capable of doing, once they had made a decision.

"Have a seat, Mr. Medov," requested the middle-aged man whose accent was easily identifiable to the agent who had spent two decades in the KGB before being given his new assignment. "He will be with you in just a moment."

Medov sat on a black leather chair in front of the large oak desk and scanned the room, admiring the many pictures of his boss posing with some of the most powerful people in the world. All smiles, of course, but Medov knew what was really lurking behind those smiles. He knew well of the big-picture agenda to organize the militant Democratic socialist groups in the United States, with the intent of creating chaos and violent protests and challenging the Democratic system, opening the door for communism.

The sound of the door opening quickly made Medov jump in his seat a bit. His two bosses entered, the heels of their shined wing tips clicking with each step. Medov respectfully rose and watched them approach him with a brisk walk and stern look.

"Minister Pavlov," greeted Medov, extending his hand, watching the man walk right by him to the other side of the desk, where he sat down, still not acknowledging Medov's presence.

"Dmitri, please be seated," offered the second man, who sat down in the chair next to him.

"Deputy Minister Vadin, thank you," Medov replied, sitting back down in his seat. This couldn't be good. Neither man had extended the courtesy of a handshake, an act he had never witnessed before. But mentally, he was prepared for anything, including a demotion, reassignment, whatever they felt was best for the cause. He knew if they were going to kill him, he would never it see it coming, so no point in worrying about it.

Minister of Propaganda, Glen Pavlov, the man behind the desk, jotted down a note on the yellow pad on his desk, then looked up.

"You have been the Deputy Chairman of the Security Council for how long now?" asked Pavlov, exhibiting an extremely unpleasant look on his face.

"Nearly one year now," Medov answered directly. "Eleven months, two weeks, to be exact."

"Yes, and in that time, have we made any progress toward our objective?"

Medov paused, realizing his work was about to be discounted, but knew it was important to state the accomplishments. "Well, yes, Minister Pavlov, we have developed a comprehensive strategy using both protestors and militarists to…"

"No! The answer is no!" Pavlov scolded, highly irritated with his Deputy Chairman. "You haven't made any progress toward your objective. At this point, we should have a strong foothold in America. We should have them on the run. Instead, two of your attack teams are in the hands of the FBI, and who knows if they will talk. Your Washington group has been obliterated. In Chicago, the protestors have been turned against our so-called leaders there."

"But in Florida, sir…"

"The Catholics!" Pavlov yelled, slamming his fist on the table, standing and looking Medov directly in the eye. "Yes, that's the one operation that seems to have succeeded. But as you know, I personally took charge of that group."

"Of course, we are all one team, working together for the cause…"

"The Americans you have recruited are inept! Incompetent! And I can't blame them. You chose them!"

Medov sat back in his chair, feeling totally overcome by Pavlov's lack of appreciation and faith in him.

The man next to him then spoke. "Dmitri, as you know, I personally chose you for this assignment," informed Alex Vadin, the Deputy Minister of Communications and longtime friend of Medov. "We are struggling to understand how you could have chosen such incompetent…"

"The students, yes!" Dmitri cut him off. "Yes, I have been quite disappointed in their lack of success. And I must tell you that I made that very clear to them recently, to the point where they understand if they don't step up and succeed, they will be dead."

Pavlov sat back down his chair and nodded his approval of that information.

"That is good," exclaimed Vadin. "But we need socialists willing to…"

"Yes, I know," interrupted Dmitri. "I will be reorganizing, bringing in militarists…"

"Like those in Washington?" Vadin challenged him.

"Well, as you know, they blew a massive hole in the side of the White House," continued Medov, watching both men nod their approval of the attack. "And that plan would have worked perfectly, had it not been for a highly skilled sharp-shooter in the Secret Service.

"Hack," Pavlov added.

"Yes, Ken Hack, the President's top Secret Service agent," Medov continued. "We didn't know he had those capabilities. Nighttime. We had the cover of the trees. Impossible!"

"Not impossible, because he killed three of your men," Vadin interjected. "And has the other two in lockup with the FBI."

"Yes, when we were planning the attack, we thought we had prepared for every possibility, every contingency. They fired those RPGs from a range of two hundred meters and with a probability of just fifty-one percent, still hit the target, which is excellent."

Vadin stood and began pacing the floor of the dimly lit office, walking over and admiring the photo of Pavlov with President Nikita Patin. He smiled, then turned. "Okay. We can understand underestimating that level of competency, but certainly never again," admonished Vadin while Pavlov watched him with curiosity, wondering where he was going to take the discussion. "And what about afterwards—and the failed attempt to use Hack's wife to take him hostage? Who was the other man helping Hack? And how could just two men take out Ivan Henry's entire group? That's unacceptable!"

Vadin walked back toward Medov shaking his head in disgust. "Dmitri, you realize that all you are offering us today are excuses," Vadin continued, placing his left hand firmly on Medov's shoulder. "You, of all people, know that we don't accept excuses."

"Who is this other man?" Pavlov demanded.

"We don't know yet, sir," Medov admitted, now feeling like a complete failure, with no answers. "We are working to find out, using our entire spy network in the United States."

"Alex, have you any information on this man?" Pavlov asked, his voice filled with frustration.

"Nothing yet, sir," Vadin said, watching Pavlov stand up, directly in front of them.

"Well, let me make this perfectly clear to both of you today," pronounced Pavlov. "I want Hack and his wife dead by the end of the week! Do you understand?"

"Yes, Minister Pavlov, by the end of the week," committed Medov. "I will see to it that there are no underestimates, no slip-ups, no issues. By the end of the week, it will be done."

"And I want those two incompetent soldiers held by the FBI dead by the end of the week. Understood?"

Both Medov and Vadin nodded. "Yes, Minister Pavlov."

"And perhaps most importantly," continued Pavlov, now pacing the floor of his office, heels clicking against the fine wood with each step, "I want to know the identity of that man that killed

Ivan Henry and his entire group. And I want him dead!" he shouted in no uncertain terms.

"Dead. Yes, Minister," agreed Medov.

"We will find him," Vadin began, looking over at his challenged associate. "Dmitri, I will need to meet with you. I will be actively involved in your efforts from this point on."

"Perfect!" proclaimed Pavlov.

"And we are going to increase our investment into these American socialist groups to ensure we have placed the proper amount of resources, as well as the right resources, behind your comprehensive plan," informed a more encouraged Vadin. "Minister Pavlov, would you like me to contact…?"

"No, I will contact Mr. Sorosky today and ask for an increase in funding," Pavlov informed him.

"Very good, sir," agreed Vadin. "Dmitri, you can wait for me in my office. I need to speak with Minister Pavlov for a moment, and then I'll be right in."

Medov stood and nodded to both men. "Good day, Minister Pavlov. You don't have to worry. We will get this done, just as you requested."

Pavlov just nodded and watched Medov exit. When he had left the room, Pavlov turned to Vadin, "Alex, I know you have a great deal of faith in Medov, but I don't want there to be any misunderstanding about my expectations."

"I fully understand." Vadin nodded.

"If he isn't successful by the end of this week… Well, you know what I will be forced to do," Pavlov continued.

When Vadin entered his own office a few minutes later, he found Medov sitting on the couch along the west wall, typing a text into his iPhone. The two men just looked at each other, knowing the next week would determine their fates.

"Dmitri, I know you have tried your best to make this work, but you know Pavlov accepts nothing less than total success."

Medov nodded. "Yes, I know."

"So we are going to get you all the resources you will need to achieve that success. Mr. Sorosky has committed as much money as we need, right from the start. So we need to determine exactly what resources we will need and how much money it will take to cover it."

This made Medov feel much better, but at the same time, he only had one week, or he would be reassigned, so he thought.

CHAPTER SIXTEEN

Dylan entered The Winery on West Madison Street skeptical about the woman who had requested the meeting through Father Quilty. She, like everyone else in Chicago, it seemed, knew Dylan was a parishioner of St. Peter's.

Father Quilty thought it strange that she would call him. Most people who wanted to meet Dylan knew all they had to do was show up at the 9 a.m. mass any Sunday. But the priest thought it important enough to pass along the message, since the woman, Robyn Kellam, claimed that she had some important information to pass along about a group that was planning a violent attack in Chicago.

Dylan had already been briefed by Captain Panozzo about his meeting with Marty Mahoney. He knew about the socialist group and what they were attempting to accomplish. Perhaps this was the same group, or perhaps it was another leftist organization. Or perhaps this woman was working for the socialists and this was a set-up. Either way, he decided to pursue it in the hopes of finding out more information.

Prior to entering the popular restaurant establishment, famous for great food and world-class music acts, Dylan took precautions, in the event this woman had set him up for a sneak attack.

He entered wearing a green chore blazer over his white collared dress shirt, blue jeans and brown chukka boots. The restaurant was only half-filled with customers, since it was only 5 p.m., too early for the full dinner crowd. Didn't matter. When Dylan walked through the front door and the maître d' pointed him to the bar, every person seated in the place suddenly turned to see him. Murmurs began. Hushed whispers spilled across the main room.

"There he is!"

"Look, it's him!"

"Should we ask for his autograph?"

A middle-aged lady and her husband began clapping. That's all it took. The entire restaurant erupted in applause. An enthusiastic standing ovation followed.

Dylan stopped, smiled and respectfully waved to everyone.

"You can't go anywhere without people cheering for you," laughed Captain Panozzo through Dylan's earpiece. "I can hear that from out here."

Dylan started laughing, then turned toward the window to see his "backup" sitting in his unmarked SUV across the street.

"Hey, you'd get the same reaction if you walked in here," Dylan informed his good-hearted Italian pal.

"I doubt it, but if you say so, that's good enough for me," Panozzo joked.

Back to business. As Dylan continued toward the bar, shaking hands with each patron and thanking them for their support, he finally saw, sitting at the bar, a blonde-haired woman who waved him over.

He wasn't certain if she was just another supporter or the lady he was supposed to meet. That was answered fairly quickly as he approached her. "Thank you for meeting me," she welcomed him, reaching out to shake hands with him.

"My pleasure," he politely accepted, sitting on the barstool next to this woman who looked like someone right off the cover of a glamour magazine. She was about 5'8" with long blonde hair, a beautiful face with big bright blue eyes and a perfect figure. She was probably about his age and looked like someone who spent a good deal of time in the gym to stay fit.

"May I get you a drink?" she politely asked, flashing a very attractive smile to Chicago's boy next door.

"Well, sure," he agreed, seeing an Irish-looking bartender step in front of him. "You don't have to get it. I can get it. Sir, can I get a black and blue?"

"Absolutely! Guinness and Blue Moon coming up," pronounced the thirty-something man of average height and build with mid-length brown hair, combed neatly to the side. As he turned to prepare the drink, Dylan turned to the mystery woman.

"So, Robyn, what's this all about? What is it you'd like to pass along to me?" he asked, watching her take a sip of what looked like a vodka tonic.

"Well, I'm a model and often receive jobs out at the Sears in Schaumburg," she began, supporting his assessment of her good looks. "And there was an employee I got to know named Ron Clapp."

"Okay," nodded Dylan, watching the bartender return with his foam-topped black and blue beer. "Thank you, sir!"

"Thank you!" replied the exuberant bartender with more than a hint of a brogue, obviously the real thing. "Great choice!"

Dylan turned his attention back to the beauty at the bar. He knew about the murder of Clapp from the information provided by Marty Mahoney.

"Well, on my last assignment just a few weeks ago, I learned that he hadn't shown up for work in two weeks, and they are unable to contact him," she continued, leaning in toward Dylan. "Mr. Reilly, I believe Ron was murdered by the group of socialists he had befriended on the CIU college campus."

Now she had Dylan's full attention.

"Ask her why she thinks that," Panozzo requested, a little too loudly, in Dylan's ear.

"He probably should have never told me about them, but I think he was trying to impress me—like he was some sort of rebel. You know, the bad boy. Some men think that's cool when they are trying to…"

"Yeah, I think I know what he was trying to…"

"Right," she laughed, realizing Dylan had followed her line of reason.

"But what makes you think he was murdered?" Dylan asked, then peeked outside at his curious police pal, who was holding a pair of binoculars pointed in his direction.

"I tried calling his number several times and would always get his voicemail," she revealed, taking another sip of her drink. "But then, yesterday, I received a call from an unknown number. I don't usually answer those robocalls, you know. But I did this time. There was a man on the other end who told me that he had received my messages on Ron's phone. He claimed to be a friend of his from CIU and that Ron had passed away suddenly. Well, I was shocked. He was young, twenty-three. I didn't think he was in bad health. I mean, he wasn't in great shape, or anything. So I asked how it happened. And the man, who probably shouldn't have shared this with me, told me that Ron had been murdered."

Silence. Dylan trying to assess her sincerity. Was she telling the truth? Or was she telling him this to try and gain his confidence, his complete trust?

"Ask her if the man said anything else," Panozzo impatiently instructed. "And watch it, Dylan. She may be setting you up."

"I am very sorry, Robyn," consoled Dylan, nodding so his friend outside knew he had gotten the message and agreed with him. "Was he a good friend of yours?"

"No, I just knew him from doing the promotions and advertisements for Sears. He would usually be there during the photo shoots."

"I see. Did the man on the phone give you any other information?"

"Thank you!" said Panozzo.

"No, he just told me that it would be a good idea not to be calling Ron's number any longer and to just forget about him. For my own safety, he added. That's what really got my attention, and it's why I contacted you. Everyone knows you're a good guy and will stand up for those who are attacked. I'm very afraid that those socialists may come after me next."

"Sounds like a story to me," Panozzo warned.

Dylan wanted to believe her story and her motives but thought it wise to get as much information from her as possible, looking for holes in the story. "When did you first meet him, Robyn?" he asked.

"Only a few months ago," she recounted.

Dylan nodded. Panozzo was in his ear, imploring him to ask if Clapp had ever mentioned a location.

"When he talked to you about this group, did he ever mention where they were located?"

"Thank you again," expressed Panozzo. "This is like 60 Minutes! You're Mike Wallace, and I'm his producer, Don Hewitt."

"It's funny you ask." She nodded and smiled. "He never gave me the exact address, or anything, but mentioned that he was heading to Wrigleyville for the meeting and wondered if I'd be interested in going to a Cubs game with him sometime. He told me that he was a big Cubs fan. He said everyone in the group was a Cubs fan. I am, too!"

"Figures!" Panozzo sarcastically quipped. "Dump her now! Next thing you know, she'll start singing that stupid song."

Dylan put his hand over his face and turned slightly to take a peek at his friend in the SUV, who was smiling and waving at him.

"What's so funny?" asked Robyn, noticing Dylan starting to laugh.

"Well, it's just the Cubs thing, you know. I'm a born-and-raised, die-hard Sox fan."

"Yeah, that's Chicago," she laughed. "You have to be one or the other, right?"

"Apparently. So listen, they obviously have your phone number and can track you down fairly easily. So yes, you need to take some precautions here. They are asking you to forget about Ron. But groups like that don't count on you to forget about what you heard or saw. They usually shut you up on their own."

"Oh, my God!" she exclaimed, fear in her eyes, now fully realizing that she was truly in danger. "I was afraid you would say something like that. What can I do?"

"Well, we need to get you out of your place and into a safehouse until we capture all the members of this group."

"Okay, yes. Sure. Anything!"

"She can stay at my house," Panozzo offered. Dylan smiled, trying to not bust out laughing at the comedy cop in the SUV.

"I have a friend, a Captain Panozzo," Dylan began, calling his Italian pal's bluff.

"No, wait. I was just kidding!" yelped Panozzo. "My wife will kill me!"

"I am going to ask him to set up a detail to move your clothes and whatever you need out of your place into the safehouse," he informed her, still not completely confident he was not being set up. "Believe me, no one can touch you there. It's guarded twenty-four seven."

"Thank you, Dylan." Robyn smiled, sliding off her barstool and throwing her arms around him, giving him the first hug he had received since his wife Darlene's funeral.

"That's alright. I'm just trying to help," he acknowledged, gently pushing her away a bit and then noticing that every single person in the restaurant was watching this scene. Smiles and curious eyes from wall to wall. What would happen next? Would he kiss her?

"Hey, maybe you should take her to your place," quipped Panozzo.

"Actually, that's not a bad idea," agreed Dylan, feeling like he would have better control of the situation, be able to find out more about her, if she were a socialist spy.

"What's that?" she asked, not knowing what he was talking about.

"Oh, I'm sorry. I just had a thought run through my head about taking you back to my place until we can get you situated. Would that be alright with you?"

A semi-devilish smile crossed her very beautiful face.

"Now please, don't take that the wrong way," Dylan pleaded, watching her smile grow wider.

"Oh, I don't mind. Believe me, honey," she encouraged, now sounding like less of a potential victim and more of the girl out on the town, looking for a good time. "What will I use for clothes? Although I do sleep in the buff, so…"

"Oh my God!!" Panozzo screamed into Dylan's ear. "Now we're talking! Man, if I wasn't a happily married man and not allowed to have any fun, I'd be right there with you, pal."

Dylan busted out laughing and tried to quickly compose himself. Robyn again looked puzzled. "Now what's so funny?" she asked.

"Well, I just don't want you to get the wrong idea," he clarified, his face dropping with the sad thought of Darlene at Good Shepherd Cemetery. "I lost my wife a year ago, and I'm still working through the pain, so…"

"Oh, I'm sorry," she consoled him, quite sincerely, recognizing that he was still in mourning. "You must have really loved her."

"Still do. Always will. She is the love of my life, to be sure."

"Okay, now you're making me feel bad," admitted Panozzo. "I'll just keep my big fat trap shut from now on."

Dylan began nodding, Robyn thinking he was agreeing with her.

"C'mon, we will get this taken care of," he informed her. "Just come with me?"

Dylan then led her out of the restaurant, which resulted in another standing ovation, but this time, it wasn't for his heroic acts the year before.

As they exited the building, he thought about how disappointed he would be if she turned out to be a spy working for the socialist group.

CHAPTER SEVENTEEN

Wooten had been to Hipsters Brew at North and Wells, on Chicago's Near North Side many times. It was known as the favorite hangout for old hippies but had evolved into the hot spot for registered Democratic Socialists of America, which had grown to twenty-five thousand dues-paying members.

He was somewhat surprised Medov had asked to meet him there, since it could pose a risk for being spotted by the FBI or Chicago Police. Wooten believed that he was still an unknown but was certain Medov was on their radar.

He had expressed his concern about the meeting place, preferring to meet once again at the Wrigleyville home provided free of charge by George Sorosky. But, for whatever reason, Medov had insisted on Hipsters Brew.

Wooten sat at a table in the back, hoping to avoid any surveillance through the colorful yellow and orange flowers painted on the front window.

Sitting down, he saw a sign on the wall next to him reading, "Favorite Table of Abbie Hoffman." He just smiled. That was two lifetimes ago, he thought, and wondered if any of the DSA kids in the place even knew Hoffman or what he had done in Chicago.

Just for fun, Wooten turned to the table of four bearded hipsters next to him and asked, "Hey, do you know who this Abbie Hoffman fellow is?"

All four busted out laughing loudly. "Yeah, we had to ask, too!" nodded one of them, holding up his two fingers, signaling *peace*. "Apparently, he was one of those old yippies from the 1960s. Other than that, we have no idea."

"Great. Thanks!" said Wooten, confirming his speculation about the hipsters' knowledge of their rebellious roots. He looked toward the door and watched Medov enter. He looked like a man who had lost his way. As usual, he was dressed impeccably in a blue Kiton suit, his gray hair slicked back, the sound of his shined black wing tips clicking with each step.

Many of the fifteen or so millennial hipsters in the coffee shop turned toward him with puzzled looks across their respective faces, wondering why this older man in a business suit would enter the establishment. Apparently, many thought he was a narcotics officer or a cop and decided it was time for them to leave.

Wooten just laughed at the sight of groups of two, three and four scurrying out of the coffee shop, looking over their shoulders to see if he was watching them. He wasn't. He could care less.

"Hello, Dmitri," Wooten said, standing to shake hands with the man whom he noticed was nearly as tall as he was, but far stronger, as evidenced by his grip.

"Good morning," the stone-faced Russian said, his accent getting the attention of the four geniuses at the next table, who decided it was also time to go. They ducked their heads downward and scampered out like four little mice, trying not to be seen.

Medov sat down with his back to the window as Kiki Krup, a silver ring-nosed, purple-haired, tattoo-laden young lady approached them with an order pad in hand. "What can I get you two gentlemen today?" asked Kiki, her dark purple lipstick accentuating a popular rebellious look reserved for Halloween only a decade earlier.

"We will each just have a cup of your dark roast coffee," Medov said, his accent also grabbling the attention of the colorful waitress.

"Very good," she said and then curiously asked, "Are you from up north, Wisconsin maybe? I noticed your accent."

"No, I'm from a little further north," he said, trying to end the conversation, looking back toward Wooten.

"Oh, Canada! Sure. I thought so." Kiki smiled, then turned,

satisfied she had solved the accent question, and walked behind the counter to retrieve their drink order.

"Not too bright," Medov commented.

"Well, they think they have their finger on the pulse, but the unfortunate truth is that they don't know shit!" added Wooten, turning to look once again at the waitress. Both men laughed as Kiki returned with the coffee and set down a full steaming cup in front of each man. The aroma of the dark roast filled the air, a wonderful smell!

"If there is anything you need, just let me know," she said, the two men nodding and politely smiling.

"Jeffrey, I had you meet me here today, because I have asked someone to join us," Medov began. "She will be here shortly. But in the meantime, I want you to know that my superiors are very unhappy with what has taken place thus far. They have now decided to take matters into their own hands and greatly increase the campaign. We have a major influx of funds and will be bringing in hundreds of demonstrators from across the country."

"Really?" said Wooten, more than a bit surprised by this news.

"Yes. Remember I told you that you are only one small piece in a major campaign to overthrow this country from the inside."

"Yes, I remember."

"And as you well know, the White House attack was the first phase of the campaign…"

"Florida, too?" he interjected.

"Yes," said Medov, confirming Wooten's speculation from the moment he had seen the news about the attack. "We are now in the process of securing the services of several hundred militia, separatists, white nationalists—anyone and everyone who is angry with America. The protests and attacks you have been part of and seen were merely a narrow attempt to cause chaos in the government and spread fear across the population."

"That's been successful," Wooten said.

"Not really. From here on, we will be increasing this effort into a major battle. We will orchestrate street battles in each of the cities we believe we can take over with protestors and our militia. Cities like Portland, Seattle, Los Angeles, San Francisco, New York, St. Louis and right here in Chicago. Those are the targets."

"That's incredible!"

"Yes, so I will need you to increase the size of your team here. And I don't want idealistic students any longer. I want killers. I want young people who know how to use a gun. I want them practiced and ready to fight. I want them to look like protestors but perform like soldiers."

"So no more supposed peaceful demonstrations?"

"That's right. When we march, we will march with weapons in our hands and destruction on our minds."

"I love it!" said Wooten. "This is great. I'm frustrated with these nitwits from CIU—except for Darius, who fits the description you just outlined."

"Yes, I agree," said Medov. "Make him one of the leaders. I have great confidence in him. The others have to go. Make them disappear, just like Clapp and…"

Medov stopped himself, knowing not to bring up the name of Wooten's dead best friend, which would most certainly sour the discussion.

Kiki the smiling waitress approached the table, holding a full pot of the rich dark roast. "Top you off?" she cheerfully asked.

"Yes, of course," said Medov.

"Toronto, right?" Kiki asked one more time, still attempting to guess his origin.

"Yes, that's right. Toronto," he said. "You know your accents."

"I don't want to brag, but I dated a guy from Toronto once, and he sounded just like you. He used to ask me if I wanted to come to his place to see his Canadian magazines. It was just a ploy to get me in… Well, you know."

The two men nodded and smiled, watching her move to the only other table in the shop that still had customers, two older hippy-looking dudes with graying long hair, blue jean jackets and worn jeans.

"Well, I have to say my superiors are quite right about American youth," said Medov. "The dumbing down of America is complete and the country ready to be taken over."

Just then, Wooten couldn't help but notice a dark-haired woman with hardened facial features, dressed in a black pants suit and matching flats. She didn't fit. What was she doing there? She looked like a lawyer. She kept walking toward their table.

"Hey, this doesn't look right." Wooten alerted Medov, who turned to see the woman approach them. Wooten grabbed his gun from his backpack. Then watched Dmitri stand and reach out to give the less-than-inviting-looking woman a hug and kiss on each cheek.

"Elaine, you look as beautiful as ever," Medov lied, then turned to introduce her. "Jeffrey, please meet Elaine Argentine."

Wooten quickly placed his gun back in his pack, stood and reached out to shake her hand. "Hello, Elaine," he said as she moved into him, giving him a kiss on each cheek, the first time in more than a decade he had received any form of affection from a woman.

Dmitri pulled out the chair next to him to seat her. "Jeffrey, I wanted you to meet Elaine, because she has a very important assignment," Medov began. "Our superiors feel very strongly about the plan I have just laid out to you, but they are still concerned about a couple of the men who have disrupted our efforts thus far."

"Dylan Reilly?" Wooten offered.

"Yes, and Ken Hack in Washington," Medov said, filling in that blank. "We have a solid plan, but we are going to need your help."

"Really?" Wooten said, happy to hear he would be part of the plan to rid the country of their beloved hero.

"Yes, they thought the little stunt killing four of our 1917 members in Washington was cute. Well, we're going to turn the table on them. Elaine is a 1917 member and knew them all personally."

"And I don't like to see my friends get killed," she said with a cold, angry look across her face.

Nods. Serious looks.

Then, Medov laid out the plan in great detail.

CHAPTER EIGHTEEN

Entering his high-security condo with his new and very beautiful friend, Robyn, Dylan wanted to be sure the doorman was introduced to her, since no one was allowed in the building unless they were cleared by Rich Kinder.

Rich was a tall man with a fairly big head, graying black hair combed to the side, wide eyes, a prominent nose and an enormously large mouth. That physical characteristic was never missed. He had learned to get past any derision by making it a running joke, showing people how he could stuff his entire fist into his mouth. That always disarmed any detractors.

Residents of the building really appreciated Rich, because he was most certainly a stickler for details. He took great pride in never allowing anyone past him, unless he was certain they were a resident, guest or approved delivery person. He had been honored as the Chicago Builder's Association 2012 National Doorman of the Year recipient, and residents knew they had the best at their front door; it made them feel a bit safer about living in their west Loop condo building.

"Hello, Rich!" greeted Dylan, reaching out to shake hands with the friendly doorman, who seemed a bit distracted by his very attractive guest. "This is Robyn. She'll be staying with me a few days. I just want to be sure you met her, so she has access to the condo and facilities here."

"Why, of course. Pleased to meet you, Robyn." Rich smiled, reaching out to shake her soft, lovely hand. "You just let me know if I can do anything for you."

"I will, thank you," she beamed, her smile lighting up the lobby.

Just as Dylan was about to step toward the elevator bank, Rich raised his right hand to stop him. "Dylan, I wanted to be sure you were aware about a young man who stopped by here earlier, claiming to be a friend of yours," Rich continued. "He wanted to go up and visit you. When I asked for his ID, he claimed not to have it with him. So I'm sorry I didn't let him go up."

"What did he look like, Rich?"

"Well, he looked to be in his early thirties, fairly short, stocky, shaved head, thick dark-rimmed glasses… You know, a guy who looks like the cover boy for Nerds of America."

Dylan and Robyn couldn't help but laugh at Rich's description of the man. But it was certainly no laughing matter.

"Were his clothes rumpled—tan khaki pants, a white shirt…?"

"Yes! That's him," Rich exclaimed, the sound of his loud voice echoing off the maroon marbled walls of the lobby.

"Okay, well, he's no friend. And I'd like to catch up with him. If he shows up again, can you please text me immediately, whether I am at home or not?"

"Oh, absolutely, Dylan. Absolutely!" he confirmed, turning to Robyn. "You know, I don't know if you are aware, but he's sort of a hero around here. And I'm pretty much like his sidekick. His go-to in case things go south."

"And Rich," Dylan interrupted, "I need you to be prepared for worst-case scenarios. Make sure you have your gun at all times, and don't trust anyone who comes in here."

A smile grew on Kinder's face. "Oh, I've got my gun at the ready, Dylan," he grinned, pulling back his red uniform blazer, revealing a shiny Smith and Wesson six-shooter in a holster. "Got one just like yours!"

"Oh, okay," Dylan replied with obvious surprise in his voice. "Well, that's good. Just be ready."

"Yes, sir, I'll be ready," he acknowledged, watching the couple walk into the elevator and go up to the seventh floor.

Over the next few hours, Dylan helped Robyn get settled in the guest room, which had very little use, except when his parents stayed with him. Captain Panozzo and a younger police officer arrived with her clothes and belongings.

It seemed that in only a short time, Dylan and Officer Greg had become fast friends with Robyn. Both were skeptical men, given their line of work, but she passed all the tests and earned their trust. After a long discussion that evening, they learned that Robyn had grown up in Northbrook and had been a competitive figure skater throughout her teen years. She had high hopes of competing for a spot on the Olympic team, until the day when she attempted a triple-axel and landed poorly, breaking her ankle. It had been the worst day of her life, she would always confide to friends and family.

After her leg healed, she tried to make a comeback, but was no longer able to leap as high and make the jumps she had made easily, prior to the injury. So as difficult as it was for her, she had hung up her competitive skates.

But the fact that she had been a skater appealed greatly to Dylan, a former hockey player. Over the next few days, they found themselves together on the Blackhawks practice rink at 18th and Jackson, just a mile from Dylan's place. It took Robyn only a short time to get her legs feeling good again, skating beautifully around the rink. Dylan enjoyed seeing how happy she was, returning to the ice. And she told him how impressive he looked skating, exhibiting great speed and power, moving around the rink so quickly.

It was a match made in ice skating heaven, although Dylan was in no way mentally prepared to get involved with another woman. His heart would always be with Darlene.

Back at his place, later that evening, he was sitting on the couch watching the news when Robyn stepped out of the guest room. She was wearing only a white cowboy hat, skimpy pink thong panties, and a lowcut top that exposed her voluptuous natural gifts. She wore Dylan's holster, hung low around her waist, his Smith and Wesson shining from her hip.

His eyes widened. Jaw dropped. He rose up quickly. Very quickly!

"Okay, pardner," said the sexy beauty, sounding like she was trying to mimic every sheriff from every Western movie ever made. "I'm going to have to take you into the pokie!"

Dylan dropped his head, laughing. He turned back toward her. No denying she was an incredibly attractive woman. Beautiful! Wonderful smile. Incredibly fit and shapely body. Beautiful olive skin. She was truly blessed.

He thought he'd join in on the fun, placing his thumbs in his front pockets like a cowpoke and walking bow-legged a few steps toward her. "Well, I guess if I have broken the law, you will have to apprehend me, eh, Sheriff?" he asked with the best Texas accent he could fake. He raised his hands, ready to be taken in for his trial.

The nearly bare-naked sheriff sauntered over, stopping directly in front of her prisoner. Gazing into his big green eyes, she announced, "Now we are either going to do this the hard way. Or the easy way."

"Well, I reckon," Dylan smiled, "I'd like to do it your way."

"Well, that would be the fun way, pardner!" she smiled, throwing her arms around his neck, then lifting up on her tippy toes to kiss him.

It was a long, soft, sensual lightning bolt of a kiss. The feel of her soft lips shot through his entire body, waking every nerve, every sense. Blood rushed to his head. All of sudden, feelings inside him that had been dormant for more than a year came to life. He was alive again.

He pulled his head back and looked into her amazing bright blue eyes. "My God, you're beautiful!" he proclaimed, feeling his emotions completely take over him. He leaned in and kissed her. He could feel the passion grow, her hug tighter, her kiss softer but firm. With her arms around his neck, she pulled herself up, wrapping her shapely legs around his waist. He could feel his gun below.

"Is that my Smith and Wesson in your underwear or are you just happy to see me?" he asked.

They laughed. They kissed again. He carried her into his bedroom, closed the door and laid her on the bed.

Loving passion filled his heart, mind and body. And there was no turning back.

CHAPTER NINETEEN

The doorman, Rich Kinder, was quite busy on this Thursday morning in early July, sorting out the mail that had arrived for the condo building's manager. As residents entered, he would quickly look up, recognize them and offer them a hearty and happy "Good morning!"

Each time, a welcome smile would be returned. The residents of the condo loved their doorman, counted on him, trusted him, appreciated his thoughtful gestures and service.

The FedEx lady arrived with a package. It was an occurrence that took place nearly a half dozen times a day from the various delivery services. Rich would normally look up to see the delivery person and say, "Good morning. You can leave that with me." He would then contact the resident to let them know they had a package at the front desk.

But this delivery was different.

"Oh, I'm sorry," apologized the dark-haired FedEx lady, whom Rich had never seen before. "I have to get a signature."

Again, this was an occurrence that happened regularly, so nothing to be concerned about on the part of the doorman. However, given Dylan's very clear direction about potential dangers and to "be careful for anything out of the ordinary," Rich was not going to handle this like a regular occurrence.

He took a good look at the woman, who was average height but thin, with dark hair, a long, narrow, skull-like face and not attractive on any level. He didn't want to be judgmental, but she was so unattractive that she was almost difficult to look at for more than a few seconds.

"I see," he responded politely, as she walked to the far end of the reception desk, farthest from the entrance. "Who is the package for?"

"Dylan Reilly," she informed him, not having to double-check the package for the name, which raised a bit of a red flag for Rich, who grabbed his cell phone from the counter in front of him, just in case he needed to send a quick alert.

"Okay, well, I have to let him know you are coming up," he said, dialing the red push-button hardline resting on the counter, then pausing a moment. "Hello. It's Rich. I have a delivery for you from FedEx that requires a signature... Okay, I'll send her right up."

He hung up the receiver, then looked at the delivery lady, his face cringing a bit at the sight of her.

"Okay, unit 711," he acknowledged, hearing something behind him. As he turned, he felt a hard blow to the back of his head. He fell hard to the floor, his head banging against the rich oak walls and down to the white marble floor. Blood appeared from the back of his head.

Standing over him was the oh-too-familiar Middle Eastern man, the angry intern, holding a Russian PSS silent pistol in his right hand. He had used the butt of his weapon to knock Rich out.

"Let's go, Raj," ordered the woman as she moved quickly to the elevators.

"One second, Elaine," he requested, looking around to make certain no one was entering, then up at the security camera and shooting his silencer to knock it out of service. "Okay, let's go!"

He quickly ducked into the open elevator with her. Within a minute, they were standing outside condo number 711.

Inside, Dylan had just showered after having a delightful bacon-and-eggs breakfast with Robyn on the deck. He was finishing getting dressed, strapping on his holster, and checking his Smith and Wesson to be sure it was fully loaded. After receiving the call from Rich, he wanted to be ready for anything.

Robyn sat in the living room waiting for him, while watching the news on WGN-TV, with the popular Gina Clare delivering the update on protests.

A knock at the door. Robyn looked over to the bedroom. No Dylan. He obviously hadn't heard the knock.

"I'll get it," she announced loudly, standing and walking over to the door. She looked through the peephole to see a FedEx delivery lady holding a white-and-blue delivery box. Dylan walked out of the bedroom and saw Robyn turning the deadbolt to open the door.

At that very moment, he received a text alert from Rich that read, *Trouble!*

"Wait. Don't...," he began, then saw her open the door just a crack, when all of a sudden, the door was kicked in, knocking Robyn backwards, causing her to fall hard onto the carpet.

Flat on her back, she watched the FedEx lady and the angry Middle Eastern intern move toward her, each holding PSS silencers. They saw Dylan to their right and turned toward him to fire.

"I wouldn't," he warned. They didn't listen. Before they could squeeze the triggers, Dylan had drawn his six-shooter and blam! Right through chest of Cruella de Vil. Blam, blam! Right through the forehead of the once-angry intern. His death stares were killed in an instant.

Dylan watched them crumple to the floor a few feet away from his new love, who scurried away from the two dead intruders. Blood was now flowing onto Dylan's plush beige carpet.

"Are you okay, Robyn?" Dylan asked, hustling over to help her up.

"Oh, my God! Oh, my God!" she kept crying out. "We could have been killed. They were trying..."

"Yes," agreed Dylan. "But they are the ones who are..."

"I'm so glad you are so good with your..."

"Yeah, I am too," he smiled, taking her over to the bedroom. "Here, just sit out on the deck. I'll get Greg to send over a unit and get this taken care of. I hope Rich is alright."

Only ten minutes later, Dylan opened his front door for Captain

Greg and a junior officer, Mike Smith, along with two staffers from the coroner's office. Dylan observed the veteran coroner technician, Skip, instruct his young lady associate, who looked like she was right out of college. He listened to the buck-toothed veteran, with a full head of gray hair, calmly talk his trainee through covering, lifting and hauling away the blood-splattered bodies on gray gurneys. As they exited, two trauma cleaning and biohazard removal specialists arrived to handle the clean-up of the blood and body fluids and sanitize the entire area.

Not a pleasant sight. Not a pleasant smell. Not a pleasant job. But they were quite proficient, eliminating any and all disease threats, making it a livable room once again.

About fifty feet away, on the deck outside Dylan's bedroom, Robyn sat on a high-backed wicker chair, taking in the wonderful breeze from the lake, while looking down at all the activities on Monroe Street, seeing several police cars and two ambulances arrive. When Dylan stepped out onto the deck, he could see she was quite shaken, crying uncontrollably, obviously overcome by the near-death experience.

Dylan surmised that the image of that evil-looking skeleton-faced woman and wild-eyed, angry man coming at her with their guns drawn must have been a visual she couldn't get out of her mind. She wiped the tears pouring down her cheeks with a napkin from the breakfast she and Dylan had just enjoyed only a half hour earlier.

Dylan learned later that the evil woman, Elaine Argentine, and man, Raj Canton, were members of the violent socialist organization, 1917. This was the same group that had tried to kill him and Ken and Elizabeth Hack in Washington.

Hearing the sliding glass door open, Dylan and Robyn looked over to see Captain Greg step onto the sturdy grey cement deck. Robyn rose from her chair, and Dylan stepped over to take her in his arms. She was sobbing, shaking, so upset.

"They were going to kill us, Dylan!" she cried, her face buried into his shoulder, tears soaking his white dress shirt. Dylan glanced at Captain Greg, wishing they could have somehow spared her from enduring the horrific experience. They had planned to move her to the safehouse a few days earlier, but she had been having such a wonderful time that she had asked if she could stay another few days. He had agreed. He felt guilty about that decision. What if she had been killed? It would have been his fault. Dylan promised himself that he would never make that poor a decision again. He wouldn't let his emotions dictate his judgment.

"I know it's terrifying," Dylan offered, to console her. "But you're alright. And you have to know I wasn't going to let another killer take another woman I love from me."

Silence. She stopped crying a moment. A smile grew on Captain Greg's face.

Dylan stood, realizing what he had just said, spoken out loud. She looked up at him, her beautiful blue eyes wet and reddened by fear. He looked at her, knowing it was a moment of truth for both of them. "You love me?" she asked.

He took a deep breath. A smile. A realization. "I wasn't sure until the moment I saw them coming through that door and I knew that I damn sure wasn't going to let it happen again," he proclaimed with conviction, determination. "Not like Darlene! I loved her so much—with all of my heart! I will never let that happen again. She was the love of my life. That was the worst day of my life. And when I saw you standing right in front of those two deranged killers, I was absolutely not going to let them hurt you."

Silence. Tears. A passionate hug. A gentle kiss.

"I have saved thousands of lives over the past year, but I have never felt the way I felt when I saved you," he confessed, feeling his heart beating, a buzzing in his head, then a courageous admission. "I didn't expect it, believe me. But yes, I have fallen in love again."

They embraced again. Captain Greg began clapping as tears began falling from his eyes. The tough, seasoned cop, who had seen so much death and destruction during his years on the force, turned away quickly, apparently trying to hide his emotional outburst from Dylan.

A few minutes later, the three were standing in the lobby, where Rich Kinder was being attended to by an attractive brunette paramedic. He was adamantly arguing that he was fine and didn't want to be taken into the hospital. She insisted that he go in for a medical examination, letting him know that he might have a concussion from the blow and that it was important that he be thoroughly checked by an emergency room physician.

"Rich, I'll stop down at the hospital later to look in on you," informed Dylan, walking next to the gurney carrying his good friend, who had revived just in time to send the text alert. "You helped save our lives with that alert. I'll never forget it, Rich."

Doorman Rich Kinder had always taken great pride in the job he did as doorman. But this was the day for which he would always be remembered. This was the day he had helped save America's hero, the man who saved thousands of lives. And now, he helped save Dylan's life.

As the ambulance pulled away, Robyn walked back toward the elevator. Dylan stood outside the front of his building and shook hands with his best friend on the police force. "Thanks, Greg. We will get her packed up and ready to go today," smiled Dylan, feeling a new sense of urgency to get Robyn to the safehouse as quickly as possible.

"It's the smart thing to do right now, Dylan," nodded his Italian pal. "If you have her ready in an hour, I will personally take her there and make sure she gets settled in."

Nods. Smiles.

"Thanks, Greg. I appreciate it," said Dylan, watching his friend step around to the side of his impressive black police Chevy SUV. "And I just want you to know that…"

Pause. Greg looked at his friend. What did he want him to know? "Yes?" asked Greg.

"I just wanted you to know that…."

"What?" asked Greg.

"I saw you crying."

"I was not!" the flustered cop shot back.

"You were. You were like a little girl, weeping. I was going to get you a tissue, but…"

"Oh, you have room to talk, Mister Kissy Face. Mister Smoochie McSmoochums!"

Laughter! Smiles! A happy moment. A bad day turned into a really good one.

CHAPTER TWENTY

Driving down 104th Avenue in Orland Park with Good Shepherd Cemetery on his left, Dylan felt conflicted, to be sure. He was making his weekly visit to the love of his life, the woman he had wanted to spend every day with until they died together, holding hands.

And here he was, only a year after she had been killed, going to her grave to inform her that he had fallen in love with another woman.

As he drove to the familiar spot along the curb to the left of the tall, impressive silver Good Shepherd statue of Jesus, he stepped out of his car and walked past the familiar graves, seeing the small Irish flag in front of brown stone with the Irish cross for William Fox and coins on the grey square stone of the gone-far-too-young Charlie Dunn.

Dylan stood three feet in front of the three-foot-tall black headstone of his departed wife, feeling like he had been disloyal to her. Cheated on her. Had he? Even polite society would say no. Regardless, he was struggling with his actions.

He had visited Father Quilty, who had told him there was no sin in starting to date another woman, but he would have to ask God's forgiveness for giving in to his passion.

"I don't know what came over me, Father!" Dylan had confessed the previous day at St. Peter's. "It just hit me. I was overwhelmed by her beauty, charisma. Her soft, passionate kisses and hugs that felt like much more than an embrace. Father, I am totally attracted to her and lost control. But I love Darlene. I will always love her. She is my wife, the only wife I will ever have."

Father Quilty seemed to be trying to help Dylan feel less guilty about his time with Robyn. He certainly knew him well enough to realize that integrity and loyalty were priorities for him.

"Give yourself time to absorb what happened to you, your feelings," Father Quilty recommended. "It may be just a reaction to a strong need for love. You know, sometimes men, and women, think they have fallen in love with someone who they barely know. And then one day, something is said or done that snaps them out of it, and they realize they don't even know the person. They wonder how they got so involved with the person. That's when they realize it was all a physical attraction, filling a void. But true love, as you well know, goes far beyond physical love. It's about going through hard times together. It's about committing oneself to the other person, even when that person makes a mistake or lets you down. It's about putting all of the other person's wants and needs ahead of your own. And that type of selflessness doesn't even take any thought. It's a natural reaction. You love them. They are the most important person in the world to you. You would do anything for them. That's what you had with Darlene. So I wouldn't get too down on yourself for having a moment of weakness. Robyn sounds like a wonderful woman. But if you really think there is more to it than physical attraction, again, I would recommend staying away from her for about six months. After that, if you absolutely have to see her, then you should. And let Cupid's love cards fall where they may."

As Dylan stood over Darlene's grave, he let the wise words of Father Quilty run through his mind, knowing he was absolutely correct. He then prayed five Our Fathers, five Hail Mary's, and a Glory Be, before talking to his wife.

"Darlene, I'm sure you know this already, but I had a moment of weakness," he began. "I know you are probably very upset with me. I'm so sorry. I don't know what came over me. But I've talked it through with that great priest at St. Peter's, and I'm not going to see her for a while. But I'm asking you for your guidance. If, for some reason, you would like me to continue my relationship with Robyn, can you give me some type of sign during the next six months? That's when he wants me to consider getting back together with her. I don't know exactly what type of sign you would give me, but in January, I'll keep my eyes and ears open. I'll pray every day.

"But know this, Darlene. I don't care if I ever am with another woman for the rest of my life. I was blessed to have you in my life. That's all I ever wanted, ever needed. So if you don't want me seeing her again, that's fine with me, believe me. I'll get over her. I'll move on."

Silence. He gazed at the writing on the stone, looking over at his place next to her.

"Now, everything I have just said may be for naught. I'm going to Washington. I've been asked to help. So the truth is, I may not need a sign from you six months from now. I may be joining you here shortly. And Darlene, honestly, that would be fine by me. I love you!"

While Dylan was at the cemetery, Captain Panozzo drove Robyn out to the safehouse in Dixon, Illinois, the hometown of Ronald Reagan. They picked up Robyn's mother in Schaumburg on the way out there, so she could stay with her daughter.

Robyn and her mother were both so impressed with the safehouse, an old white wooden framed home with a white picket fence, sitting along a tree-lined street that looked like an American town. A 24-hour guard would be stationed outside the home for the foreseeable future, until the terrorist threat had ended. They certainly didn't want to see Robyn or her mother hurt by this vicious group of killers.

"Now, you call me any time of day or night," Captain Panozzo told them both. "We have a great system set up here, and believe me, you will be guarded, and you will be safe."

He watched a lovely smile cross Robyn's face, her mother looking at her daughter with pride, knowing she had made a courageous effort to help the police find the terrorist group responsible for attacking the White House.

The first day in Dixon, they took a tour of President Reagan's childhood home. It seemed fitting.

CHAPTER TWENTY-ONE

After witnessing their former associate and friend, Ron Clapp, shot in cold blood and stuffed in a trunk, Ramirez, Slagle and Kamus were none-too-eager to return to the Wrigleyville home.

When Wooten group texted them to meet there, they didn't respond immediately. The three talked privately at the campus library, where Marty Mahoney spotted them. The redhead ducked out of sight, behind the row of history books. He peered through two old hardback books that had a putrid smell, *To Kill a Tsar* and *The Death of Caesar*.

The redheaded freshman watched the three stooges have a loud and animated discussion. They were so loud, he could actually hear them arguing about going back to the Wrigleyville home. Mahoney couldn't blame them for that strong instinct. He certainly would never go back there.

He listened to them agree about a plan to only meet Wooten in a public place, so he couldn't shoot them. Slagle proposed they ask him to meet at Hipsters Brew, a place they were well-known and felt safe. Smiles. Nods.

Ramirez typed something into his phone, most likely a text. He looked up at his two friends, chatting about possibly bringing a gun with them. Where would they get one? Ramirez listened, then looked back down at his cell phone and read the screen.

"Okay. Thursday, ten a.m. at Hipsters," he agreed, pressing the thumbs-up over the message. "And yes, I agree. I've got a gun, and I'll bring it, just in case."

The Three Commiegos stood and exited the library together,

while Mahoney texted Captain Panozzo about the meeting. He quickly received a reply.

Thanks Marty! Meet me at headquarters at 9 a.m. I'll take you over there.

Two days later, Wooten entered Hipsters Brew and spotted his three socialist trainees at the back table, the same place he had just met Medov and the now-deceased devil lady.

"I'm glad to see you boys," welcomed Wooten, sitting in the corner chair, facing the window. "This won't take too long."

Curiosity, confusion, skepticism. What did Wooten want?

Parked across the street from the shop on Wells sat a black unmarked police SUV with Captain Gregory Panozzo and his new sidekick, Marty Mahoney. The captain had a high-powered camera, which was able to capture clear images of the four men sitting at the back table.

Panozzo watched the purple lipsticked waitress, Kiki Krup, with her prominent silver nose-ring, purple hair, and tattoos from neck to toe, approach them, take their order and cleverly place a bug under the center edge of the table, just as Officer Greg had asked her to do. Well, it was really less of a request and more of a paid gig. She had received $200 for simply placing the miniature transmitting device under the table without being seen. She might have been a rebel, but as she told the friendly policeman, the Gothic Girls concert was coming up, and the money would help cover the ticket costs for her and girlfriend, Tonia. She added that they would have sold their souls to see the concert and hear the group's two big hit songs, "Devil" and "Whore's Song." Who wouldn't?

When the Gothic Girls' biggest fan returned with the pot of coffee and poured each of her four customers a fresh cup, the conversation between them was coming through loud and clear in the police vehicle outside.

"We are going to be making some changes in the organization," the tall, thin, balding thirty-something informed them. "Now, I want you to know that we have appreciated all you have done for the organization—recruiting students, leading the attacks at the protest, all of it. Great! But from this point on, Tim and Robert, we are no longer going to need your help. You can just go back to college and lead a normal life. You don't have to worry about overthrowing America any longer."

Through his binoculars, Panozzo could see a surprised look on the two college students' faces. From what Marty had told him about Wooten's pronounced rule of never being able to leave the organization, this get-out-of-jail-early offer must have raised a great deal of curiosity and skepticism.

"Wait, what?" asked a perplexed Slagle, sounding completely taken aback by this news. "What do you mean, you don't need our help any longer? And what about Ramirez?"

Wooten paused a moment, knowing full well he would get that question. "We are going to need Ramirez. He has an athletic skillset that will be of value to the movement. I think you are well aware of his abilities. But from this point on, the organization is going to be focusing on Washington and enlisting the support of socialists who are prepared to bring violent protests, men who are willing to kill for the cause, willing to kill anyone at any time."

Ramirez leaned back in his chair, looking over at Slagle and Kamus, mouths agape, eyes wide, looking greatly concerned. Officer Greg knew they were certainly happy to hear they were no longer needed in a group that killed its members in the blink of an eye, but this wasn't consistent with the lifelong commitment rule.

"How exactly do I fit in with that description?" asked Ramirez, who also wanted out of the organization. "I have no intention of killing innocent people."

Silence. Wooten, with an intense look, leaned over the table, trying to intimidate Ramirez. "This is a lifelong commitment, Ramirez," he informed him once again.

"What about Tim and Robert?"

"They're out!"

"What about the lifelong commitment?"

"We're making an exception. But you're in, like it or not. Understood?"

Kiki returned with her pot of coffee. "Back with the dark roast you boys love so much. Can I top you off?"

Silence.

"Okay, I'm sorry. Was I intruding?" she asked, sounding defensive.

A cold stare from the balding Democratic socialist.

"Right. Well, I'll be back with your check, then," she politely replied, then walked away quickly, nervously.

Ramirez, never one to be pushed around or threatened, leaned right back over the table into Wooten's face. "Well, I don't like it!" he proclaimed with a fierce look on his face. "And I'm out as well! Get my point?"

Just then, Wooten felt the muzzle of a Glock gun shoved hard into his jewelry case. He tensed up and leaned back, not wishing to have his family gems left as a tip. "Oh, okay, okay, okay!" he pleaded. "I didn't know you felt that strongly about it. Don't shoot, please!"

Ramirez pulled the gun back from Wooten's trophy case.

Panozzo looked at Marty. "If he shoots, we're going in," he informed his young friend, who felt special, like he was now a member of the police force, although he was really just signed out as a ride-along.

Wooten sat back and motioned with his hands, trying to visually calm down Ramirez. "I guess I'll have to let Mr. Medov know that I have made three exceptions and we won't need your help any longer as well. Sound good?"

Silence. Ramirez staring daggers at a man for whom he obviously had no respect or trust. "Yeah, it sounds good." He glared, a low harsh tone in his voice. "And I know where you live. I know your family's address in Evanston. Understand?"

Wooten nodded.

"And I've got friends who I'm going to share that information with, just in case you or one of your hired guns decides they want to pay any of us a visit. Clear?"

Nods again.

"Medov, too! Anything happens to any of us, and one of my pals places a letter in the mail, detailing the actions of Medov and you at the Wrigleyville home."

Wooten's face grew stern, staring daggers at Ramirez.

"So this is it. I don't ever want to see you, or hear from you, again! Ever!" Ramirez announced, pushing back from the table and standing up from his chair.

Slagle and Kamus watched this exchange, looking surprised. They might have known their college friend was most certainly the bravest, strongest and most capable. But now he was standing up to Wooten and the Russians. This display of courage was impressive to all watching and listening, including the two men in the police SUV outside.

Slagle and Kamus stood and followed Ramirez out the door, looking empowered but equally scared. Ramirez had just pissed off the Russians!

CHAPTER TWENTY-TWO

The Cathedral of St. Matthew the Apostle in Washington, D.C. always felt like a safe haven for Ken and Elizabeth Hack. Parishioners only knew them as the attractive couple that sat in the fourth row from the front, on the right side of the main aisle, for 10 o'clock mass each Sunday.

On this sunny Sunday morning in the third week of July, kneeling with praying hands, the White House Secret Service Director prayed for God's guidance and support as the United States was about to enter into a battle against domestic terrorists unlike any fight the country had ever encountered. He knew all too well, as did his beautiful wife, that they might not survive this war. They might die and were eager to make certain they had everything in order, including a trip to the confessional the day before.

They knew the drill. Both had been in this position before, during their three tours of duty, fighting a vicious and dangerous enemy, the Taliban in Afghanistan and al-Qaeda in Iraq.

Those days had helped them to love and respect their country even more. They had been in places where people didn't have the freedoms offered in America. Seeing the brutal treatment so many people suffered in countries run by dictators and monarchs made freedom a sacred word in the Hack household.

They believed American freedom could never be underestimated or underappreciated. They were never disheartened by news reports detailing the treasonous actions and volatile words of some who claimed to be Americans, merely because they were naturalized citizens. Watching those ugly reports, the couple knew that those people would have greatly benefitted from serving their country in foreign lands, just as they had done. But unfortunately, they would never sign up for that life's experience, which would expand their knowledge of the world and perhaps help them appreciate the many liberties represented by the American flag.

Ken and Elizabeth Hack knew those freedoms were worth fighting for to the death. This had been the belief shared by hundreds of millions of brave and patriotic Americans for more than two centuries. It was shared by the people filling the pews that Sunday morning.

Like Ken and Elizabeth, faith, family and love of country were the priorities for the twelve hundred Christians, both registered and visiting Catholics, meeting their Sunday obligation, honoring God.

It was 9:30 a.m., and hundreds streamed into the large bronze doors of the impressive red brick Cathedral, some stopping to admire the beautiful church and the mosaic above the door, with an image of St. Matthew holding his gospel.

Designed by architect C. Grant La Farge, the Cathedral had been built in the form of a Latin cross. The interior was richly decorated in marble and semiprecious stones, with large translucent alabaster windows. No one entering the doors could miss the magnificent artistry throughout the sanctuary. It was a sight to behold.

On this morning, many visiting Catholics were seen standing in the main aisle and looking up at the impressive octagonal dome, which extended one hundred and ninety feet high, with a ten-foot crucifix at the top. Then, a few began pointing toward the front of the church and an expansive altar with a white marble table and a thirty-five-foot mosaic of Matthew centered behind it.

Certainly, the Hacks, like any of the regular parishioners, were aware that the Cathedral was something of a tourist attraction. Visitors were exposed when they walked up to the foot of the altar to take a photo of the circled designation where President John F. Kennedy's casket had rested during his funeral mass on November 25, 1963.

Ken was great admirer of JFK's positive and encouraging words and hope-driven leadership, and he always appreciated the opportunity to receive Holy Communion on that historical remembrance each Sunday.

It was almost 10 o'clock. Ken had finished his prayers. He sat down in the pew and looked back at the entrance to see if the procession had lined up, ready to begin. Seeing the look of the people around him, he marveled at the respectful Americans, dressed appropriately for the celebration of mass in God's house.

On display were pretty summer dresses, colorful heels, polo shirts, dress shirts, khaki pants and shined shoes. After all, this was the Cathedral. Reverence to the Lord was always required, but somehow, the average Catholic would feel more compelled to dress accordingly when they entered the rich grandeur of such an impressive church.

As always, the Hacks looked sharp. Ken was dressed in black slacks and a soft blue polo shirt, exhibiting his tanned, muscular arms. Elizabeth's long brown hair was draped over her shoulders, and a lovely light pink mid-length dress accentuated her long, tanned legs and bright pink heels. They were mostly certainly a very attractive and impressive-looking couple.

"Please stand for our entrance hymn, 'Onward, Christian Soldiers,'" said music director Steven Thomas as the powerful tones from the Lively-Fulcher Great Organ boomed across the ornately decorative walls of the large and impressive house of worship.

Ken and Elizabeth rose, holding their blue hymnals and singing a song they loved.

Down the middle of the main aisle emerged Grand Knight Edward Amato with five Knights of Columbus, dressed in full ceremonial uniforms. All watched the impressive parade of men in their black tuxedos with the KoC emblems on their left breast pockets and white sashes across the fronts, red capes, white feathered chapeaus, and silver swords to their sides, always ready to defend the faith. They were proud Catholics dedicated to charity, unity, fraternity, and patriotism. JFK had been a Fourth Degree member.

The six devoted men led the procession of altar boy, Tommy McKay, holding a large dark brown wooden cross high. He was followed by his twin brother, Johnny, Deacon Vince Roberts and Reverend James Reynolds, each with reverent praying hands. It was a beautiful sight.

The throng of joyous, singing faces in the pews turned to see God's soldiers, twin altar servers and the Apostles' representatives as they passed. Smiles.

After the opening prayer, Ken couldn't help but grin upon seeing a familiar face, a great friend, walk up the four steps to the white wooden podium for the first reading. Elizabeth turned and nudged Ken, a shared moment of happiness and pride for them.

A murmur grew, whispers, pointing fingers, craned necks, all surprised to see the lector, Dylan Reilly.

"A reading from the book of Isaiah," Dylan stated in a strong, confident tone, which demanded the full attention of all in the church.

"Behold, all of those who are incensed against you shall be put to shame and confounded; those who strive against you shall be as nothing and shall perish. For I, the Lord your God, hold your right hand, it is I who say to you, 'Fear not, I will help you.'"

As Dylan read the inspirational words, Reverend Reynolds beamed at the beautiful delivery of the man the world had come to know for his great courage. And here he was, in the Cathedral of St. Matthew, reading about having the courage to turn away from fear and believe that God was always with us. Some had their cell phones out, taking photos of Dylan during his reading, realizing that he was a guest reader and might never be back.

After reciting Isaiah's prophetic words, Dylan turned and descended the steps to his chair on the right side of the altar, directly across from the two thirteen-year-old twin McKay boys dressed in white surplices over black cassocks, the standard vestment.

The acceleration of a car, then squealing tires erupted outside. Irritated frowns filled the packed sanctuary. Annoyed parishioners looked toward the holy art of the stained glass windows.

The choir director, Jill Mather, then led the congregation in the responsorial hymn, "A Psalm of David." A full choir backed her beautiful voice, with a small orchestra of horns and strings filling the hearts, minds and souls of all in attendance. How could one not feel the Holy Spirit, standing in such a beautiful cathedral, surrounded by respectfully dressed parishioners, listening to such heavenly music?

But then, a horn honked. A car peeled out. The church walls couldn't defend the peaceful sanctity of the moment from the intrusions of the outside world. More irritated frowns. Father Reynolds grimaced his displeasure.

A few minutes later, Dylan finished the second reading, St. Paul's First Letter to the Corinthians, calling on Christians to be strong and courageous. He closed the Bible and placed it on the shelf of the podium, as was the procedure for lectors at every Catholic church in the world. He then looked out at the congregation, seeing six Knights of Columbus lined up along each wall closest to the altar, standing guard over the holy proceedings.

Dylan smiled and returned to his seat.

That was the cue for Deacon Roberts to stand and walk over to Father Reynolds. The deacon bowed his head to the priest who blessed him, then walked to the center of the altar table, bowed, and kissed the Bible. He lifted the good book high and walked up the steps of the podium. The music to Alleluia streamed through the long golden pipes of the magnificent organ, accompanied by twelve hundred voices singing to the glory of God.

Their heavenly voices muffled the sound of trucks screeching up to the front of the church.

"A reading from the Holy Gospel according to Matthew," said

the tall, sandy-haired forty-something Irish deacon dressed in white albs with a colorful green stole over his left shoulder that hung down to his right side. "And do not fear those who kill the body but cannot kill the soul; rather fear him who can destroy both soul and body in hell." Deacon Roberts concluded the Gospel reading. "The Gospel of the Lord!"

"Praise to you, Lord Jesus Christ!" bellowed out a chorus of voices in unison.

The deacon closed the Bible and walked down the steps.

Suddenly, loud banging, shouts, a commotion coming from the narthex. Nearly everyone in the pews turned simultaneously toward the entrance. What was happening?

Screams! Shouts! A gunshot! A loud scream! Two ushers in their uniformed blue blazers sprinted in through the side doors.

"It's them! It's the killers!" shouted one of them. "They shot Bill!"

Darting eyes. Mouths agape. Shrieks of fear. Anxiety everywhere. Thoughts of running.

Dylan ran to the middle of the altar. "Everyone, get down on the ground now!" he ordered. Men, women and children quickly dropped to the floor, hiding under the cover of the wooden pews. Dylan waved for the priest, deacon and altar boys to run into the sacristy for cover.

Ken and Elizabeth Hack remained cool and calm. Their survival instincts took over. They grabbed their .357 Magnum Smith and Wesson Model 19 revolvers and stepped into the side aisle, behind three of the Knights. All six defenders pulled from their black blazers their issued Glock 43 single stack 9mm pistols.

Ken hurried around the front pew to the center aisle, while Elizabeth stayed with the group of Knights along the west wall.

Then, bursting loudly into the church from the three entrances, came six rough-looking, angry, stubble-faced large men in tan camouflage military fatigues. They were each carrying AR-15 semi-automatic rifles.

At each entrance stood a pair of the killers, shoulder-to-shoulder, ready to massacre innocent, peace-loving, faithful Catholics. They were the same domestic terrorists from the Florida massacre, but had added two new thugs for the bigger assignment—to kill Ken Hack and his wife.

At once, the six intruders scanned a seemingly empty church, seeing only six Glock-laden Knights, two .357 Magnum-wielding Hacks and an unknown man with an old six-shooter in a holster strapped to his right leg.

Surprise erased the anger off the faces of the hoodlums.

Recognizing the situation, an evil smile grew on the face of the leader, known by his men as El Maton.

"Stay here," he ordered the man next to him, then started walking slowly down the center aisle. "Oh, so you're ready for us? Is that it?" he laughed, directing his comments toward the unknown man with the six-shooter, who was standing at the foot of the altar over JFK's emblem.

Dylan's arms hung straight down. Right hand next to his brown leather holster and pearl-handled shiny silver six-shooter.

"Where's Hack?" El Maton barked at him.

"Right here!" yelled Hack with his .357 Magnum pointed directly at El Maton, who laughed at Hack's bravado. Then, he looked back at the man with the brown wavy hair. He squinted when he realized who he was looking at.

"Are you that guy?" he asked in a low tone of curiosity.

"Yeah, I'm that guy," Dylan replied, opening and closing his right fist, loosening it up for the battle.

The news seemed to get the attention of El Maton's five associates, who most likely knew what Dylan Reilly could do to them. A few looked like they were ready to run, until their leader looked back at them.

"You stay and fight, or I'll kill you," he demanded of them.

Then, the oxycodone-addicted, sick and twisted murderer

looked back at Dylan. Would this maniac try and prove he could outdraw the The Fastest Gun?

El Maton glanced over at the sharpshooting sniper, Ken Hack, down on one knee with the Magnum resting on the first pew, pointed directly at the evil man standing in the entrance. Dylan could easily see the eyes of El Maton. He was very obviously high on something. Did he really think he could shoot him and then Hack? Did he really think he was that good with his semiautomatic weapon? Dylan just shook his head at the killer's drug-induced confidence, thinking no one could stop him.

"You're all going to die!" El Maton announced to the faithful.

Gasps emanated from under the pews. Pleas for mercy, "No! No! Please don't!"

El Maton flashed his delight.

"Not today, hombre!" yelled Dylan, signaling for the Knights to get in their three-behind-three shooting formation, as directed and practiced during training sessions following the Florida massacre.

Like a well-organized unit of U.S. Marines, the Knights snapped into formation, guns drawn and pointed at the enemy. The Glock 43s were trained on the evil-minded men who, ironically, were now standing inside a monument to a faith that preached love and peace.

The brave Knights could not turn the other cheek to this group. It was not an option, because that would most certainly be a death sentence for the twelve hundred innocent lives cowering under the pews. Yes, this was certainly a time when Just Defense was necessary, taking the sword Jesus had offered his Apostles the second time he sent them out.

El Maton glanced at his men, who seemed to realize that they had just walked into a Catholic turkey-shoot. But now, with guns pointed at them, especially The Fastest Gun, they didn't seem quite as eager, quite as motivated, to kill the Hacks and other Catholics whom they had expected to be unarmed.

"Don't even think about it!" yelled the evil leader, realizing his men might turn and run. Suddenly, anger and panic were evident in his eyes. "Kill them!" he shouted and started to run toward Dylan with his rifle pointed directly at him. Before he could take a second step, a silver bullet from a famed six-shooter tore into his heart, while a golden bullet from Hack's .357 Magnum penetrated the center of his head. The force of the bullets sent him flying backwards, his head exploding against the back pew. His lifeless body flopped hard onto the red carpet floor. Dead!

At that moment, all six Knights opened fire on the other five combatants, killing three of them before they could fire their weapons. Two others, the new men, ran out the door, with Elizabeth and two Knights chasing right behind them. Loud explosions from a .357 Magnum and Glock guns blasted outside the church.

A few moments later, two brave Knights emerged behind Elizabeth, victorious smiles providing the update. By this time, the parishioners had risen from under the pews. Some were sitting, crying. Some standing, talking. Most were watching the final scene.

Elizabeth walked to the west wall, where Dylan and Ken stood over one of the attackers, still alive, although severely wounded, having taken six bullets to the abdomen.

"Why did you this?" demanded Ken, angry that they would try to massacre Catholics again. "Who's behind this?"

"We're here to kill you!" barked the bloodied marauder, watching Father Reynolds approach. "You think you've won. You don't know what's about to hit you!"

Murmurs. Gasps. Mouths agape, eyes wide. What did he mean?

As the attacker lay on the floor, bleeding profusely, struggling in great pain, he somehow managed to grab a pistol from the pocket of his camouflage army jacket. He tried to lift it toward Hack, who quickly kicked it out of his hand. The bleeding criminal's arm dropped back to the ground, his final shred of energy spent.

"We're going to need an ambulance," Dylan said to Ken, who nodded in agreement, hoping to keep the criminal alive in order to learn about the Florida attack.

"Is that everyone, Grand Knight Amato?" Hack yelled back to the Knights of Columbus leader.

"Yes, sir," he responded.

"Great! Folks, you're safe now."

The few still hiding under the pews rose to their feet. They were most certainly shaken, some crying uncontrollably, but they were alive, and only one usher had been injured but would survive the injury from a bullet to his upper right shoulder.

Applause began and increased across the spacious room, everyone so happy they were safe. They were alive. Unharmed! They had been saved by Dylan Reilly, Ken and Elizabeth Hack and the Knights of Columbus.

They were so grateful! They began chanting, "Knights! Knights! Knights!"

Ken, Elizabeth and Dylan could only smile as they shook hands with the brave men of the Knights of Columbus.

They talked about the wisdom of the leadership of the Catholic Church in America deciding, after the Florida massacre, to place the Knights in charge of protecting churches across the country. That was when the organization had drafted a Just Defense Plan, preparing every chapter for the worst-case scenario. It was that decision and that plan that had saved twelve hundred Catholic lives on that sunny Sunday in July. It was the first test, and the Cathedral chapter had performed courageously, setting the standard for the Knights across America.

"We are going to clear the Cathedral," Ken Hack announced. "Just please follow the directions of the ushers and Knights. For those who would like to meet, Father Reynolds has invited all of you downstairs for coffee and donuts. It might be a good idea, given what you have all just been through."

A half dozen police cars screeched up to the front of the famed religious building. Six of Washington's finest jumped out of their vehicles and began the protocol carried out at every crime scene.

While two cops cordoned off the steps where the two dead men lay bleeding, two others ran inside to take care of the others.

The gray van from the coroner's office arrived a few minutes later, two staffers ready to haul away all five dead bodies, once the police had finished their investigation.

Hoping to spare the faithful the disturbing sight, the staffers placed sheets over the three dead men bleeding a darker color of red into the carpet. The fourth severely injured man was quickly placed into an ambulance by two female paramedics, who wheeled him off on a gurney.

A flow of Catholics descended the steps to the basement, where they would share their thoughts and emotions to help dissolve their anxiety a bit.

Only a few walked straight to the parking lot and travelled home, getting as far away from the traumatic scene as possible.

After the church had been cleared, Ken, Dylan and Elizabeth approached the Knights who were standing in a group, talking, shaking hands, feeling victorious, having saved so many lives.

"You men were tremendously courageous today," said Ken, shaking the hand of a very relieved Edward Amato, a fairly tall and handsome, blonde-haired, blue-eyed Grand Knight. "I hope you will communicate your success with the other chapters, so they can feel confident about your plan. I would think the chances of this happening again are slim, but you never know. That's the problem."

Nods. Pats on the back. Smiles. Congratulatory comments everywhere.

Father Reynolds stood with the Hacks and Dylan, watching all of the commotion. "What did he mean when he said, 'You don't know what's about to hit you'?" asked the priest, who obviously was hoping nothing further would happen to his parishioners or any innocent people in the D.C. area.

Ken placed a supportive hand on the worried priest's right shoulder.

"It was just another empty threat, Father, just trying to continue scaring people," said Hack, who actually knew exactly what the killer had meant but chose not to place any more fear into the priest or his congregation.

"Well, I guess that's somewhat encouraging," said Reverend Reynolds. "Will you all join us downstairs? I'm sure everyone would love to meet you."

"I don't think so, Father," said Dylan. "This is really the shining moment for the Knights of Columbus. It would be better if everyone understood that they were the defenders and we just happened to be here to help."

The priest smiled and nodded. He heartily thanked each of them one more time, then descended the steps to give his homily about courage, which would now have a much greater meaning for his grateful flock.

CHAPTER TWENTY-THREE

Hundreds of Harley-Davidson cruisers roared down Interstate 70.

High handle-barred choppers streamed down Highway 95.

Roadsters sped up on Route 66.

American flags flapped violently from the back of each thundering hog.

The sights and sounds of an army of powerful motorcycles dominated the streets leading to the Capitol of the United States, Washington, D.C., on a muggy Thursday, July 23rd.

As these magnificent two-wheeled vehicles streamed inside the 495 beltway, onlookers stood and pointed. It wasn't Memorial Day, when the Capitol was accustomed to seeing this type of loud, colorful parade.

Nonetheless, hundreds of pedestrians, with their collective mouths agape, stopped to take photos of this spectacular sight, listening to the rolling thunder stream down Pennsylvania Avenue, presenting an assortment of fashions and images.

Some men were dressed in leather from head to toe. Others had short-sleeved shirts exhibiting their large, tanned, muscular arms. A large number had U.S. military veteran emblems on their navy blue caps or green fatigue jackets.

Beards were everywhere. There were long, scraggly black beards; shorter cropped brown beards; salt-and-pepper old beards. A ten-year-old boy pointed at one man who stood out. "Look, Mom, no beard," he said, watching his mother's amazement at the one biker who had actually shaved his face clean and smooth. The biker turned and smiled at the pointing lad and his pretty mom, who was wearing a yellow mid-length summer dress.

Everyone watching marveled at the scene. There were sunglasses, lots of cool-looking shades. There were tall black boots, multi-colored bandanas and helmets. Leather, plenty of leather, and a few biker chicks holding on tight from behind. There were large duffle bags strapped on the backs of some riders, obviously packed for a long trip.

This was not the whole picture, for hidden under those packs were a variety of semiautomatic rifles, Glock guns, ammunition, grenades and RPG-7 launchers. It was a clever display of creative packing, hiding such a large amount of firepower.

Above flew two Bombardier Challenger 650 jets racing toward the same destination for the same purpose.

This was an unusual scene, to be sure. It was most certainly a dangerous arsenal of hidden military might, carried by a motorcycle army comprised of seemingly zealous nationalists.

Anyone viewing this display would believe they were looking at a band of patriotic brothers traveling to Washington, D.C. to exhibit their pride in America.

But they would be wrong!

For this long line of flag-waving patriots was assembled by none other than Jeffrey Wooten. He had been greatly inspired by Dmitri Medov, who had informed him that he needed to assemble an army of six hundred of the most vicious leftist thugs he could find to attack the Capitol Building. And if he failed, both of them would be dead before the end of the week.

That was plenty of inspiration for the outcast from Illinois.

With the personal stakes so high, Wooten worked directly with Medov to carefully plan every detail of the attack, taking into account each potential scenario, drawback, challenge and outcome.

During the two-week planning process, Wooten was quite happy to learn that they were being provided with an unlimited budget from George Sorosky to carry out the terror campaign. He was also given direct contact with the leaders of each Democratic socialist terrorist chapter in America, including the infamous 1917 group. These leaders were the same men who had transitioned peaceful protests into violent riots in Portland, St. Louis, Chicago, New York, Kenosha, cities all across America.

They were experts at weaving themselves into peaceful demonstrations, and then in the blink of an eye, inciting violence. They chanted manifestations of hate and rage, threw rocks at the police, set businesses on fire, and encouraged others around them to do the same.

It didn't take Wooten long to assemble his all-star group of six hundred leftist thugs, all rebel socialists to the core. They were society's biggest losers, miscreants, drug pushers, sex offenders. Many were hardened criminals, killers and psychopaths, who represented the type of citizens that socialism would generate if it became the government in America.

As Medov and Wooten had sat in the hotel restaurant late Friday morning, awaiting the army of bikers to arrive, the Russian leader had stressed the importance of each man fully understanding his role in the campaign.

"We must present them as loyal and devoted Americans who would give their lives for the country," explained Medov, who was less concerned about the bikers grasping that concept than he was about selling this ruse to the FBI, Secret Service and police. "The training and experience of those agents and the cops makes them skeptical about everything. But if they believe they are actually looking at a massive group of patriots, that should help lower their guard just enough so we can hit them with a surprise attack."

Would they believe that this well-organized, perfectly presented group of false patriots was just another one of the many conventions meeting in the nation's capital? Would they make any connection between this group of conservative patriotic bikers and a contingent of Democratic socialist protestors? If they were skeptical, Medov hoped they would prepare for a clash between the two ideologically opposed groups and be totally unprepared when the leftist, and supposed conservative, patriots joined forces to attack the Capitol Building.

Surprise would be essential to achieve success.

It was just before noon when Medov and Wooten watched the bikers pour into the parking garages of the four-star hotel. Medov knew the authorities would immediately notice that this was not a typical destination for a bikers' convention. This was most definitely not the usual clientele of these high-end hotels, to be sure. The sight of thousands of Harleys in the multi-deck parking garage inspired some passersby to take a quick iPhone photo or two. The local police didn't miss it. But they knew the story—biker convention.

Medov and Wooten did everything possible to sell the event as a legitimate convention. Fake brochures were created and placed on a phony website, just in case the authorities wanted to check it out further.

Inside, there were fake seminars conducted in conference rooms, with a hundred paid actors posing as bikers and watching PowerPoint presentations about motorcycle safety, how to best mount your flag, and the ten best pickup lines to meet a biker chick.

The biker narrative was sound, but Medov and Wooten didn't want to chance having no other protestors show up. So those same "biker convention" actors were costumed and prepared to play protestors during the attack. They were given signs to hold up and lines to memorize, shouting out patriotic slogans as they marched toward the Capitol Building:

- *America, Love it or Leave it.*
- *Send all Commies Back to Russia.*
- *Stand for Your Flag*
- *In God We Trust*
- *Faith & Family, American Values!*

To encourage the greatest performance from these actors, they were told it could be their big break—the magic words for any actor hoping to hit it big.

Preparing for every possible scenario, the actor-protestors were prepared with talking points if approached by a news reporter. If someone asked who was organizing the protest, they would answer, "True Americans!" If asked who was paying the bill for this very costly protest, again they would answer, "True Americans!" If asked who headed the organization, the answer would be, "People who love this country!"

If successful, Medov and Wooten believed they would be orchestrating the biggest deception in American history. And one that would make their Russian bosses very happy.

While the fake presentations were taking place in the conference rooms, the real education was taking place in the large suites where the plan of attack and assignments were being laid out in great detail for the bikers and the real protest leaders.

"Think of this as a combination of the most famous socialist attacks in history," said Wooten, with Medov standing to his left. "We will be dropping firebombs from planes, like in 1921. We will have a passionate speaker inciting the mob, like at the Haymarket Riot. And we will have protestors like at the 1968 Democratic Convention in Chicago. But we will be adding our own historical tactic to the history book, with six hundred patriotic-looking bikers armed with semiautomatic weapons speeding toward the Capitol Building and shooting every cop and politician in sight."

Wooten looked out at his nodding audience, who seemed quite impressed by this strategy. "And when it's over," he continued, "There will be dead cops and Senators littering the streets and halls of Congress. Flames will be shooting from the roof of the Capitol Building. We will blame all of this violence and destruction on the cops, the FBI, the Secret Service, who were shooting innocent patriotic Americans. We have influential political leaders in the House of Representatives and Senate, who will back all of this up for us.

They will take the lead in calling for major change in America, saying it's time to pronounce America a country of Democratic socialists!"

Loud applause erupted. Smiles everywhere. They were going to actually change America, just like Vladimir Lenin and the Bolsheviks had changed Russia in 1917.

Medov took a good look at the group in front of him. These were men who had made their marks, had earned their communist medals, and had been handpicked to lead the members of their socialist chapters to Washington. They would be leading an army of violent socialist protestors, attacking the Capitol Building and shattering America's confidence in the government's ability to protect them. They would scare citizens from coast to coast. This was no longer just one city for these men. They would now be on the national stage, doing their damage, which was the great appeal for each of them.

Wooten brought the meeting to an end, and the room cleared.

"Well, this is it!" Wooten said to his Russian boss. "We know the situation and our fate if we fail."

He left Medov's suite, both men fully understanding what had to be done.

There could be no more Chester Walling screw-ups on Lake Shore Drive; no more Ivan Henry debacles; no more Elaine Argentine failures.

And, as had been clearly pointed out to him a few days earlier by Minister Vadin, no more El Maton moments. Vadin had told Medov, in that short and curt phone conversation, that he had to beg Pavlov for one more chance, telling him it was the oxy-addicted El Maton's fault completely. He pointed out to Pavlov that at least they now knew who was helping Hack—Dylan Reilly.

And that vital piece of information had saved Medov and Wooten's lives, at least for one more week.

However, if they didn't succeed with this plan, they knew an asset would be sent to kill them both.

CHAPTER TWENTY-FOUR

When the sun rose on this particular Saturday morning in D.C. and President Fallon looked out of his bedroom window in the White House, it most certainly looked like it would be a beautiful day.

But not far from him on this fateful Saturday, others had a different forecast in mind.

A heavy mist hung over the Potomac River as a blitzkrieg of motorcycles broke through the fog, roaring over the Theodore Roosevelt Bridge.

Fierce, helmeted warriors tightly gripping their handlebars, eyes focused straight ahead, semiautomatic rifles hidden under the bags strapped to the pillions of the bikes.

The black leather-vested leader, Dmitri Medov, riding an impressive gray Harley CVO, thrust his right hand forward, signaling the direction for his army, then sped down Constitution Avenue. The Stars and Stripes waved mightily on the flagpoles centered at the rear of each powerful machine, making the event look like a patriotic parade as they passed the south side of the White House.

A few miles later, the long line of two-by-two cyclists split into separate streams, with the leader of the second group, Tim Kamus, veering right down 4th Avenue on his candy apple red touring bike.

As Medov's group drew closer to the battlefield, he quickly raised his right hand high. Hundreds of bikers behind him slowed. All eyes were on their leader. He checked a text he had received from Jeffrey Wooten, who was with hundreds of protestors, marching in front of the Capitol Building.

The reassigned Chicago protest leader had arrived an hour earlier and was surprised to find more than four hundred men and women, all angry socialists, young and old, who were ready to join the fight. This unexpected turnout, resulting from one Tweet on social media, led Wooten to give his backup protestors, the one hundred hired actors, the opportunity to stay and fight, or leave. Leave was the choice for every one of the paid pretend demonstrators.

Walking off the set, as they described it, they whined nonstop about the poor production and their loss of the IMDB credit. Meanwhile, the real protestors were handed signs that read:

We Love America!
Land of the Brave!
Four More Years
We Love Fallon!

They held their signs up high, laughing at the deception. Wooten smiled. Everything was in place.

For the four Capitol Police atop the steps, protecting the famed domed building, this group was not like the usual protestors who rallied near the White House or Capitol Building. Quite noticeably, they were not all young college boys and girls, who would normally be holding up BLM signs, anti-gun signs, anti-American signs, and even pro-socialist signs.

No, this seemed to be a group of patriotic Americans who loved their country so much that they would make the trip to Washington to voice their support. A few years earlier, that would have been a red flag for the police. But in 2015, it was just another day in D.C.

As Medov's group approached 3rd Avenue, he held his arm up high again and came to a complete halt on his Harley. He turned around and looked back at the long line of young and middle-aged men ready to do battle. So many of them had travelled a long distance for this fight. They would not be deterred.

He texted Kamus. "Ready?"

"Ready!" was the reply from the leader of the second group, which had come up Independence Boulevard on the south side of the Capitol Building.

More than two hundred yards in front of Medov's group, hidden from the protestors, FBI SWAT Tactical Commander, Dirk Williams, and National Guard General, Jerry Lewandowski, surveyed the enemy through their binoculars from the rear of the large formation of officers and soldiers.

Up above, inside the Capitol Building, FBI and Secret Service agents were stationed, in case any protestors broke through the line. FBI Director Sheldon Phillips coordinated the efforts of his teams from a SWAT armored vehicle parked in front of the Supreme Court Building.

On the Senate side roof of the famed domed building, Ken Hack and Dylan Reilly lay flat, with sniper rifles pointed at the leader of the cyclist army.

"Medov?" questioned Hack, not certain if the man under the helmet was the Russian they had been tracking for so many years.

"Yep, that's him," said Reilly, who had received the FBI's thoroughly researched report on the longtime Russian assassin.

"But who's leading that other group?" Hack wondered.

"Oh, that's Tim Kamus, one of the protestors from Chicago," Reilly informed him, having received that tip from his Italian pal back in the Windy City.

The CIU student Kamus had double-crossed his two friends, Ramirez and Slagle. After the Hipster's Brew meeting, he had contacted Wooten to tell him that he wanted to be part of the mission. Despite Ramirez's effort to save him from possible death, Kamus thought that participating would elevate him in the new socialist order, once they took control in America. Anyone who knew Kamus would laugh at his decision. He was flunking most of his courses at CIU, but he thought he was smart enough to become one of the leaders in a new socialist America.

The army of cyclists and protestors was now in position for the major assault. Each knew their actions would one day be detailed in history books across the globe.

Medov's group was a few hundred yards west, on Constitution Avenue. Kamus' unit was parked on 1st Street, across from the Library of Congress. Kamus would storm in from the east on Constitution. And Wooten's protest group—all armed, locked and loaded—would charge right through the middle and up the steps of the Capitol Building.

Medov was confident the three-pronged attack, plus air power overhead, would succeed. The timing was arranged to attack the Capitol Building once the planes had dropped their firebombs on the roof of the House of Representatives.

The rebel soldiers sat on their hogs, took out small American flags and began waving them, saluting the Capitol dome and singing "God Bless America." They would play their patriotic role of deception to the hilt, until it was time to attack.

Commander Williams smirked under his binoculars, watching this performance of the group on Constitution, mentally giving them two thumbs down for bad acting.

"Take em' out," Medov ordered, watching each of his soldiers pull out their weapons from under the large black bags covering the pillions of their cycles. Kamus' group was doing the same on the east side.

At that moment, two sleek, tan Bombardier Challenger 650 jets appeared in the distance, descending quickly toward the Capitol Building. Medov and Kamus smiled, knowing their great battle, their moment of honor, was just about to start.

"This is the tower. Please identify yourself," said Alfred Soldatz, a highly experienced Air Traffic Controller at Reagan National Airport. "You have entered a Flight-Restricted Zone. Please identify yourself."

"Oh, geez. Hey, dare," said the pilot, Marc Ruffino, with a thick

Wisconsin accent. "Cripe, we must have taken a wrong turn. We are so sorry."

"Turn around immediately. You're in FRZ!" demanded the highly decorated Vietnam veteran, who had no problem turning his fighter jets loose when necessary, to stop any unapproved aircraft in FRZ.

"Hey, don't ya know, I'll do my best," Ruffino said, laughing to himself, although Soldatz could clearly hear, as he watched the high precision jet stay on course.

"Turn around immediately!" Soldatz yelled. "Last chance!"

"Hey, dare. Kiss my ass!" said Ruffino, a die-hard socialist from Kenosha, Wisconsin, as he moved closer to the Supreme Court Building, which was the first strike on his plan of attack. Dismissing the warning, he flew directly over the Supreme Court Building and dropped a fairly large incendiary bomb onto the roof.

Inside, only seven staffers and one Supreme Court Justice had arrived early for work. The bomb exploded directly above the chambers of Justice Rebecca Gorshinsky. She never knew what hit her and suffered no pain as she was blown to smithereens, her legacy now painted across the walls of her office. Fortunately, the seven staffers were able to escape.

"Oh, dat was a beaut, don't ya know!" said Ruffino, smiling wide, having accomplished his first assault, as he turned his jet toward the Capitol for his second strike. The former hairdresser was so thrilled with himself that he didn't see the F-15 Eagle zoom in behind him. That was when Ben Stevens, the top gun in the Naval Air Force, launched an AIM-7F/M Sparrow missile.

Ruffino heard the missile fire and could see it coming at him in his mirror. "Oh, cripe!" Ruffino blurted out, his last words.

A direct hit! A huge fireball filled the blue morning sky.

The explosion was so loud it shattered the glass of several buildings below. Stevens peeled off to avoid the fireball from the explosion, which rained fire and metal onto Lower Senate Park.

"Dat was a beaut, too!" quipped Soldatz, now the one laughing to himself.

A half mile away, the other Bombardier jet sped toward the White House, which was still under repair from the RPG attack a few months earlier.

"Turn away immediately, or you will be shot down!" ordered Soldatz.

"Hey, man. Like, sorry," said the pilot, with an accent from the valley in Los Angeles. "Like, I've lost all direction here. Dig?"

Before he could find out if the dark-haired Vietnam Vet who had fought on Hill 225 dug his lost directions story, Ben Stevens flew in directly behind him, while an artillery group at the White House lined up the hostile L.A. flyer in their sights.

Simultaneously, the National Guard below fired a hypersonic Mach 5 hypervelocity projectile from their Paladin howitzer while Stevens launched another AIM-7F/M Sparrow missile.

Seeing the missiles coming at him, the L.A. pilot tried to quickly veer his plane hard to the left. Not quickly enough. The two deadly missiles simultaneously arrived at the center of the Bombardier, creating a massive explosion!

Fire and metal rained down onto the South Lawn of the White House. Guardsmen ran for cover, avoiding the falling debris. Luckily, none were injured.

Seeing the two explosions, it was decision time for Medov: Run or fight?

"Saddle up!" yelled the Russian, all three hundred of his men pulling out a variety of semiautomatic weapons, jumping on their starter pedals, creating a universal roar as they fired up their powerful machines. Then, Medov opened up his throttle and darted quickly toward Constitution Boulevard and the Capitol Building.

On the west side, Kamus mirrored Medov's every move, as instructed during their two-hour planning session the day before, at the four-star hotel.

It was an amazing sight! Two long lines of powerful American flag-waving motorcycles, speeding two-by-two toward their destination.

"Hold your fire until I give the word," said General Lewandowski, who then announced over a sound system, "You are unlawfully carrying firearms on the grounds of the U.S. Capitol. Drop your weapons, raise your arms and surrender."

Medov's mouth dropped, his heart raced. The entire plan depended on a sneak attack, and somehow, that had been thwarted.

They would have been wise to abort the mission, living to fight another day. That was not an option, however, for the Russian who would be killed if he didn't follow through with the plan.

Just then, the five FBI SWAT armored vehicles and ten tan High Mobility Multipurpose Humvees, with M2 heavy metal machine guns, sped to the front of the Capitol Building, creating a roadblock. They formed a solid barrier from east to west in front of the protestors, who watched in dismay. Behind them, more than five hundred National Guard soldiers and one hundred FBI SWAT Tactical officers lined up, locked and loaded with Colt M4 Carbines.

"What the hell!" griped Wooten, looking at an unexpected army of trained and experienced soldiers with semiautomatic weapons pointed in his direction. The Guard and SWAT teams set up a seamless perimeter, prepared to stop the attack with tremendous firepower and weaponry. Williams and Lewandowski thought the sight of the soldiers behind the machine guns in the turrets of the Humvees would be enough to deter the misguided lefties.

Unfortunately, they were wrong.

"Anyone runs and I'll shoot you myself," Wooten announced, deterring the quick escape many had been considering upon seeing the line of military vehicles.

Medov's motorcycles sped closer to the center of the Capitol. The befuddled protestors heard the roar and turned to see them coming, giving them some hope.

Wooten, like Medov, knew he had no choice. If they ran, death was a given.

"Weapons!" Wooten yelled, and the large group of supposed peaceful protestors whipped out Glocks, AR-15s, AK-47s. They were staring at a line of tan army vehicles and black armored trucks blocking their path to the Capitol steps, although a moment before, they thought they would easily be running up and into the Capitol building.

CHAPTER TWENTY-FIVE

In the Longworth House Office Building, Speaker of the House, Fritzi Bello, was working to get a jump on key legislation that would be introduced on the floor of the House of Representatives later that week.

That morning, Ken Hack had briefed her by phone about an impending attack on the Capitol Building by a large group of Democratic socialists. Upon hearing this warning, she had just smiled. "Democratic socialists?" she asked. "They won't attack us. That you can count on!"

Frustrated, Hack threw his hands up in the air and desperately tried to appeal to her common sense. Very calmly and nicely, he said he would send over two of his agents to help escort her safely from the Longworth Building.

"No" was the answer, once again.

He tried ordering her to leave. She laughed.

"Well, I'm going to keep two Secret Service agents outside your door," he informed her. "When the attack occurs—and believe me, it's going to happen—they will lead you out of the building to a safe place until it's over."

"You're funny!" said Bello, still not taking Hack seriously. "You'd better tell Senator Calvin Huster as well. He's here, and we will be meeting in my office in an hour from now."

Totally exasperated, Hack radioed two more Secret Service agents to guard Senator Huster and escort him out of the Hart Senate Office Building.

When the two agents arrived on the third floor outside of the Minority Whip's office, they received the same level of stubborn stupidity that Hack had endured from Bello. "We're Democrats!"

Huster had argued, looking out his office window, where he had a view of the large group of protestors at the front of the Capitol. He couldn't see the Humvees and armored SWAT trucks in front of them. "And if they are Democratic socialists, then we are all in it together, right? Look at those peaceful protestors out there. It's freedom of speech in action. I love it!"

Just then, Huster's attention was diverted by a twin engine jet flying toward the Capitol.

"Time to go, sir," said agent Denny Perme, who grabbed the Senator's arm and forcefully led him out of his office, down the hall and toward the elevator bank. Only a minute later, they were down the elevator and exiting past the security guards. As they emerged from the building, they all quickly looked up when they heard a loud explosion. Then, they watched a large fire coming from the roof of the Supreme Court Building, a long thick plume of black smoke pouring out of the roof with a jet plane just beyond it.

Suddenly, Senator Huster wasn't quite as confident about the peaceful demonstrations. Agent Perme led him away from the Hart Building. Walking briskly, the three men continued to watch the private plane fly off in the distance.

Then, a fighter jet appeared right behind it. The jet's powerful thrust created a sound that pierced through the sky and echoed off Washington's famous buildings and monuments.

George Washington would smile. Freedom was being defended.

Huster had never heard a missile being fired until that moment. He stopped to watch it shoot across the sky so fast. A direct hit! A massive explosion. The plane was completely blown apart. A large fireball of wreckage rained down.

"Oh, my goodness!" said the Senator. "I guess this is an attack. I hope no one below is hurt."

From her office, Bello witnessed the same scene. Now she, too, was convinced that Ken Hack had been right and that she should have listened to him.

The two Secret Service agents led her out of the Longworth

Building. She gingerly stepped over shards of broken glass covering the cement sidewalks and street. The explosion shattered many of the windows in the government buildings around the Supreme Court.

She took out her cell phone and called Senator Huster. "I'll meet you in the Rotunda in a half hour," she said. "We have to do something about this. If Americans find out this was done by Democratic socialists, we're done. I'll have Senator Thompson meet us there as well. This is his fault!"

CHAPTER TWENTY-SIX

Despite the construction being done at the White House to repair the major damage from the RPG attack in May, President Jack Fallon was sitting in the kitchen, ready to have his breakfast, as was his usual routine.

After a loud debate with his trusted Secret Service Director, Ken Hack, he had moved back into the White House in the middle of June, not wishing to allow that cowardly attack to take the leader of the free world away from the center of power, where Americans were accustomed to seeing him. He knew it would bring them more comfort and confidence. Every poll taken supported his thinking, in regard to the decision to move back.

In early July, when Hack had briefed him about reliable reports of an impending attack on the Capitol Building, Fallon had stubbornly refused to sit in the bunker until it was over. He had been through so much worse in his life, so many battles, surviving a sadistic, torturous prisoner of war camp for five years. Plus, he had the National Guard working with the Secret Service to protect the White House. In his mind, that was all he needed to thwart an attack.

On this Saturday, July 25, Congress would not be in session, so the Capitol Building was virtually empty. Nonetheless, the symbol of American power would be protected at all costs.

Despite the warning from Hack, Fallon, admittedly a very stubborn man, planned to get in a round of golf at Andrews Air Force Base. Somehow, despite the briefing he had received, he just didn't believe there would actually be a major assault on the Capitol Building.

So he attempted to approach this day like it was business as usual at the White House.

Four Secret Service agents milled about the kitchen. Agent James Hicks, a Medal of Honor recipient who had served with valor in the Iraq War, was watching out the window. The President sat drinking a cup of mild Columbian coffee while reading *The Washington Post*, complaining to the First Lady, Carol Fallon, about the negative coverage he always seemed to receive, regardless of how many good things he was doing for the country.

"I'm telling you, Carol, if I win a second term, I'm going to set up a standards and practices division to oversee the news media," he told his wife, who had been through thick and thin with him, including an affair he had had with a fashion model that had nearly broken up their longstanding marriage. "These quotes from anonymous sources, and the editorial commentary in the reporting, has to stop. People don't know what to believe anymore."

She nodded politely, aware that this was his biggest pet peeve, dating back decades, to when he was first running for Senator in the U.S. Congress, and *The Washington Post* continued to hammer him for his failings as a husband and father. He never forgave them and never granted an interview to anyone associated with the *Post*.

Just then, a loud roar coming from outside the White House diverted their attention.

"This looks like the start of it," said Agent Hicks, a look of determination now on his face, knowing he must get President Fallon to the Presidential Emergency Operations Center. "Time to go to the bunker, sir."

The President stood and quickly walked to the window. His face cringed in dismay, and he nearly dropped his favorite white "Commander in Chief" mug.

"Wow! That's it?" he asked, looking out at a long line of powerful motorcycles driving down Constitution Avenue.

"That's it," said Hicks.

"Are you sure that's not a parade? Look at the American flags on the back. Carol, is there a parade scheduled today?" the President asked.

"I don't know, Jack," said his wife, who walked up next to him to see what he was talking about. "Oh, that's quite a line of patriotic cyclists, isn't it?"

"Those aren't patriots, ma'am," Hicks informed the First Lady. "That's their attempt to try and throw off the police so they can conduct a sneak attack. I promise you there are weapons under those packs on the back of their cycles."

"Is everyone in position at the Capitol Building?" asked President Fallon.

"Yes, sir. Just talked with Ken. They're ready for 'em."

"And we've got a perimeter set up by the Guard outside the White House, right?"

"Yes, sir. More than three hundred soldiers."

"Well, then, let's have breakfast!" Fallon said, smiling, knowing he had nothing to worry about.

"But, sir..." Hicks began and was quickly cut off.

"You like extra bacon, right, James?" the President politely asked, watching exasperation cross Hicks' face.

"I do. I love extra bacon, but today, I'm going to just stand here, if you don't mind, sir," he said, watching the President walk back over to the kitchen table, where one of the White House staff was delivering the sumptuous bacon-and-eggs breakfast.

The longtime married couple, who had become a point of pride for millions of Christian Americans who believed in marriage until death, just as Jesus had taught, sat eating the wonderful breakfast prepared by White House chef, Jacque LeCuc. Halfway through the meal, they both became distracted by the sound of a plane overhead.

"Hey, we got a problem here, sir!" said Hicks, seeing a Bombardier Challenger jet crossing into the FRZ and flying toward the White House. "Time to go, everyone! Let's go!"

Hicks led the president, Carol, the staff and Secret Service agents out of the kitchen and down the steps. He wasn't going to take a chance with the elevators, in the event they were bombed.

The buzzing from the plane grew louder.

"We got a plane coming at us here," said National Guard Sergeant Jim Moore from the front of the White House.

"We see it," said Hicks. "On our way down to the bunker."

"Should we shoot it down?" the Sergeant asked.

"Yes," said Hicks, not blinking an eye about knocking out a plane flying over the White House.

"Copy that!" Sergeant Moore confirmed.

"C'mon, let's go, let's go!" Hicks encouraged, as they all quickly ran down the hall, going directly down the corridor leading to the high security elevator. When they reached the red doors, Hicks pressed the button and the doors opened immediately, just as a loud blast was heard outside the White House. Then, another one from above. Then, a massive explosion that was so strong it shook the entire building.

"Get in!" yelled Hicks, and everyone hustled into the large elevator.

Outside, the guard had shot down the plane, and a large fireball rained debris onto the South Lawn of the White House.

Sounds of men yelling, running, the crash of something large.

"Watch out! Run! Look out!"

Hicks listened to it all, hoping nothing would land directly on the White House. The elevator doors opened, and out they all scurried behind Hicks, who quickly typed in the code and placed his thumb on the identification device. The doors opened, and into the bunker they went, feeling a great sense of relief.

A few minutes later, Hicks heard Sergeant Moore ask, "Everyone okay?"

"We are all good!" said Hicks, looking at the President and his wife standing with the three Secret Service agents who were watching the monitor, which showed the smoke and debris across the grounds of the White House.

"Any more planes?" Hicks asked.

"No, I think that's it, sir," said Moore. "We fired our Howitzer just as an F-15 launched its missile. That was quite an explosion!"

"Sure was," smiled Hicks. "Sure was."

CHAPTER TWENTY-SEVEN

Commander Dirk Williams looked out at more than four hundred armed and dangerous militia moving on foot, along with six hundred enemy combatants on motorcycles, blaring in from the east and west.

It was a virtual stare-down between the now-obvious violent protestors and five hundred National Guard and FBI SWAT Tactical officers. Williams wondered if they would now withdraw, since the surprise attack had been squelched.

No such luck!

Wooten stood at the front of the pack, squeezing his rifle, breathing heavily, working up his courage. Williams may have known about the attack, but he didn't know there was no turning back for Wooten and Medov.

"Let's go! Fire! Fire! Fire!" Wooten yelled, then opened up his AR-15 on the tan-and-black perimeter of heavy vehicles. His militant army followed his lead, firing their weapons toward the soldiers and SWAT teams who seemed to be fully protected by their heavily armored tactical vehicles.

"Charge!" yelled Wooten, running toward the barriers, while firing his semiautomatic rifle.

"Fire!" yelled Commander Williams from the back of his forces. The SWAT officers opened up on the invading Capitol Building raiders.

"Fire!" yelled General Lewandowski, allowing his soldiers stationed behind the Humvees to open up on Wooten's army, hitting the invading socialists with a heavy barrage of fire power. The M2 machine gun took out forty of them in less than twenty seconds.

One of the casualties was Jeffrey Wooten, who took two bullets right through the center of his head from the sniper rifle above, held by Ken Hack. Wooten fell lifeless, dead before he hit the ground. His miserable life had come to an end.

Most of the protestors were too busy fighting and dodging bullets to notice. The few who did see Wooten go down, took off running in the other direction, hoping to live another day.

SWAT officers and soldiers kept firing, protestors dropping, bleeding.

Their return fire ricocheted off the heavy metal armor of the trucks and Humvees. One of the soldiers manning a machine gun was hit and fell into the Humvee, where he was immediately treated by one of the medics.

Just then, from the west came the rolling thunder of the socialists led by Medov.

"Fire!" yelled Medov, his riders steering with one hand while shooting their rifles with the other.

General Jerry Lewandowski yelled out, "Ten o'clock! The cyclists! Fire!"

His highly trained soldiers turned their attention to the motorcycle corps and hit them with a stream of bullets, hundreds of rounds fired all at once.

Bikers speeding in fast were hit one after the other, pelted with bullets, thrown to the ground. Motorcycles careened across the pavement, their riders flying alongside, out of control. Wave after wave were shot, killed.

Further enraged, snarls grew, firing wildly, recklessly, aimlessly. Filled with vengeful thoughts, none of the protestors feared death any longer. This was their last stand. This was the fight they had hoped to win over many years.

Just then, from the east, Kamus' core of cyclists came flying in at high speeds.

"Shoot! Keep shooting!" yelled Kamus, exhibiting bravery he had never shown before. "Fire! Fire! Fire!"

A few of the SWAT officers were hit. Medics attended to them immediately, just like on an Iraq battlefield, where most of them had served. The firing continued.

Cyclists dropped. Protestors fell dead. Soldiers were wounded, some killed.

Screams! Shouts! Fearful eyes. Bloody bodies. Red pavement. Anger everywhere.

From the roof, Dylan Reilly and Ken Hack lay side by side with their sniper rifles, picking them off one at a time. Between them, they killed more than fifty of the marauders in two minutes' time. They didn't miss.

The SWAT team then launched tear gas, creating a haze of green smoke across the front of the Capitol Building.

With no gas masks, the socialists threw everything they could at the soldiers—hand grenades, Molotov cocktails. Explosions and fires erupted all along the base of the Guards' perimeter. Cyclists and protestors began passing out from the gas.

Suddenly, one hundred yards in front of the Capitol, two white vans sped in, screeched to a halt. The side doors opened. Two RPG-7s were launched right at the center of the National Guard perimeter. A large explosion. Two Humvees flew fifteen feet in the air. Soldiers flying, many killed. Both army trucks destroyed, fires blazing from the wreckage.

Hack and Reilly watched from above.

Then, a man emerged from each van with an RPG launcher. The men ran a few yards to spots where they had a good view of the entrance to the Capitol Building. They each got down on one knee, aimed and…

"I've got the left," said Hack. Blam! Launcher dead!

"I've got the right," responded Dylan, who fired one round, a direct hit to the chest. The launcher falling from the dead man's hands.

The two drivers began speeding off, trying to escape.

"Vans!" yelled Hack.

"Got it!" said Dylan. Both men shooting the gas tanks of the fleeing vehicles, creating blasts that sent the trucks flying, landing on their sides, burning.

The drivers survived, jumped out and tried to run.

"Nope!" said Hack, who a put bullet in each of their legs, leaving them screaming and moaning in pain.

The scene was total chaos. Green smoke everywhere. Army trucks burning. Soldiers and SWAT officers dead or injured, sprawled across the pavement. Bikers and protestors scattered across the grounds of the United States Capitol Building.

Through the mist, Medov spotted the opening in the middle and raced through it on his gray Harley, with six others right behind him. Kamus saw him and darted through as well. They found the cement ramp on the side and raced up to the top of the Capitol steps.

"Ken, you see them headed up the steps?" Director Phillips radioed.

"We got 'em! Thanks!"

Reilly and Hack jumped up and ran for the elevators.

Four Capitol Police and three FBI agents, all dressed in full riot gear, were positioned at the top of the steps.

"They're coming at you, Jamal!" said Director Phillips, alerting his agents. The FBI's Jamal Gage turned to see the terrorists coming up quickly and shot two right off their bikes. The dead men fell off their motorcycles and rolled down the steps of the Capitol, leaving a trail of blood, their driverless bikes bouncing all the way to the bottom.

Medov, an Olympic rifle champion, reached the top of the steps. He jumped off his bike, ducked behind it for cover and took aim. Kamus and the other two attackers were right behind him and did the same.

A firefight ensued. Shots bounced off of the large, heavy metal cycles.

The sharpshooting Medov took aim. Blam! Down went one cop. Blam! Two.

The two remaining police and three FBI agents fired from behind the large Capitol columns.

Agent Gage fired, missed. Fired again, hit Medov in the left arm, the Russian falling backwards to the ground. Kamus fired and wounded Gage, who fell to the floor and took cover. Despite the pain, Gage quickly worked to reload his gun,

Medov looked down to see a haze of green over the U.S. soldiers and SWAT police as they continued fighting it out. Protestors lay dead everywhere.

Medov knew he couldn't stay there. He had to move and move quick.

CHAPTER TWENTY-EIGHT

Two Blackhawk helicopters buzzed toward the Capitol Building. Director Phillips wanted to end the battle on the Capitol steps immediately and had called them in.

Soldiers inside the helicopters spotted the six combatants at the top of the steps. They were ducked down behind their motorcycles. The highly experienced soldiers opened up with their machine guns, spraying bullets, killing two of the invaders. Medov, Kamus and two others survived and weren't going to give the Blackhawk soldiers another stationary target.

With adrenaline pumping through them like electricity, they jumped on their bikes and sped into the entrance of the Capitol Building, bullets flying all around them.

Safely inside, Medov arrogantly popped a wheelie in victory. Kamus, right behind him on his touring bike, mimicked the leader and pumped his right fist in the air, shouting, "Yes!"

The two others followed them on their sleek black Cobra 4s, up to the famed Rotunda.

Medov, old and hurting, crawled off the seat of his Harley and announced, "We are in charge now!

At the corner of his eye, he saw someone approaching. He quickly grabbed his rifle and turned to find the Speaker of the House, Fritzi Bello, and Senate Minority Whip, Senator Calvin Huster, approaching him.

The smiling Bello attempted to be diplomatic during this highly dangerous situation. She smiled and said, "Welcome to the Capitol Building. We are the leaders of the Democratic Party, which I know you support."

An evil grin grew on the Russian's face.

"There's a lot at stake here today, with your attack, since you represent the Democratic socialists," she continued, oblivious to the reality of the armed and trained enemy assassin standing in front of her. "I thought we could go to my office and talk about it. I've got cookies—chocolate chip!"

Medov just laughed, then lifted his AK-47.

"Wait! We're Democrats!" Bello pleaded.

The bullets tore through the weak, flabby body of the eighty-year-old, jolting her back several feet to the ground. A puddle of red quickly formed. Shock filled Huster's face. He turned tail and ran, wishing he had listened to the two Secret Service agents who had ordered him not to go there.

Medov shook his head at the cowardice of one of the most powerful men in Washington. Then, he pulled a .357 Magnum from his leather vest pocket, lifted it and fired one shot. A direct hit. Huster's head exploded! His headless body bounced off the ground twice before finally resting.

As Medov tucked his gun back into his vest, Kamus and his two surviving crew members stood there perusing the Capitol dome above the famed Rotunda. That was when two familiar Americans ran in, barely out of breath.

Ken Hack was holding his .357 Magnum, and Dylan Reilly had his famed six-shooter holstered at his side.

"Drop the weapons," Hack ordered them loudly and clearly.

A sneer grew on Medov's face. He turned toward the two men, his AK-47 in his right hand, pointed downward at that moment.

"Drop them, or I'll drop you!" Hack ordered, gaining the attention of Kamus, who wanted to take that offer, realizing they were now in an unwinnable situation.

"I won't ask you again. Drop your weapons," repeated Hack, now pointing his rifle directly at Medov. Then, all of sudden, a shot from behind tore into Hack's upper right shoulder, jolting him forward, his .357 falling to the ground.

Dylan quickly turned to see the old, decrepit Senator Lenny

Thompson, a well-known socialist but now an American traitor, standing with a smoking musket in his right hand. As he tried to load another metal ball into the muzzle of his Revolutionary War-era weapon, Dylan drew and fired one shot, sending the musket spinning several feet away.

Then, he spun to see the four men pointing their semiautomatic rifles directly at him.

He dropped to the ground and rolled quickly to his left, bullets bouncing off the floor to his side. He lifted himself up, fired. Down went one. He rolled right, gunfire all around him. He was in serious trouble, and he knew it. For the first time, he didn't know if he would survive.

Then, all of a sudden, a shot came from the side. Down went another of the terrorists.

From the floor, Dylan looked up to see a very familiar face, Sergeant James Henry, the man who had taught him how to use a gun—and a sniper rifle, just a few weeks earlier.

Medov quickly turned his rifle toward Henry, but before he had squeezed the trigger, Dylan shot the gun out of his hand, watching it spin behind him.

Kamus then raised his gun at Dylan. A shot rang out from behind. Kamus was jolted forward. His face numb, he fell to the ground. Dead!

Wounded FBI agent Jamal Gage appeared. Dylan smiled.

Medov was the lone assailant, surrounded. He reached in his pocket, grabbed his Magnum and turned toward Dylan. It was a face-off that had to happen.

"Don't do it!" Dylan warned, watching Medov's eyes narrow. As the Russian assassin raised his gun, Dylan, once again and with lightning-fast speed, drew his Smith and Wesson six-shooter, and blam! blam!—two shots—one through the head, one through the heart.

All watched as Medov dropped face-first to the floor. His life was over. His mission was over. His attempted coup of the U.S.

government was over.

With all threats gone, Dylan looked toward his friend. "Ken, are you alright?" Dylan asked, seeing his buddy in great pain on the floor.

"I'm good," Ken said, Dylan helping him up to his feet. "What did he shoot me with?"

"That, my friend, was a ball and pen musket shot!"

"A what?"

"Senator Thompson is either old enough to have fought in the Revolutionary War, or he just keeps muskets in his office."

Even in pain, Hack couldn't help but laugh at the thought of being shot with a musket.

Commander Dirk Williams and a dozen of his FBI SWAT team members came running up the steps. "Everything good here?" he asked, seeing the dead bodies on the floor.

"Yes, sir, Commander Williams," said Hack. "Just one traitor to take into FBI headquarters for interrogation."

Williams looked at the sullen Senator Thompson, "Can't say I'm surprised. Glad we finally got 'em."

Smiles and nods all around.

FBI agent Gage slapped the cuffs on the old man, who had once run for the highest office in the country. Now, he would be tried for treason and most likely hung.

Thompson looked down at Medov, who had assured him that his plan of attack was completely foolproof. As it turned out, it was completely foolish.

What Medov didn't know was that one seemingly harmless meeting at Hipsters Brew in Chicago was where his plan had fallen apart. Wooten had revealed enough information about the Washington attack, and it had been heard by a Chicago Police Captain via a bug placed under the table by a purple-haired, nose-ringed waitress named Kiki who would do anything to see her favorite band, Gothic Girls. Who wouldn't?

Jamal Gage led Thompson toward the main entrance of the

building, with Hack and Reilly walking a few feet in front of them. As they descended the steps, the green smoke below had all but dissipated. But in the mist, they could see the figure of a man standing with something on his back.

"Hold it," said Dylan, raising his right hand, his instincts once again taking over.

Then, a loud sound emanated from the spot where the man was standing, like a sandblaster. All of a sudden, the man began rising in the air. He had a jetpack strapped to him. As he rose higher out of the green, the rifle he was holding became visible. "Down with America!" he yelled and opened fire.

Dylan, with lightning-fast speed, drew his six-shooter and blam! A silver bullet right between the eyes of the flying attacker, who fell immediately to the ground, splattering across the cement pavement.

Sighs of relief. Glances below to see if there were any others.

"You are fast!" said Thompson, who had watched the exhibition of speed right in front of him.

"Taught him everything he knows," laughed Sergeant Henry, placing his right hand on Dylan's shoulder. "I think you've gotten even quicker."

"Well, I do what I can," Dylan laughed, walking down the steps with his three pals.

It was learned later that the jetpack man was Robert Slagle, who, like Kamus, had decided to double-cross Ramirez. It was the classic socialist move, the double, double-cross.

Back in Chicago, Ramirez watched the report on the news and just shook his head in complete amazement and total disgust at the stupidity of the two CIU students and wannabe socialists whom he had tried to save.

CHAPTER TWENTY-NINE

FBI Director Phillips had an extensive file on Dmitri Medov and had been tracking his movements throughout the United States for years. Phillips strongly suspected he was working with a rogue group of KGB agents out of Moscow but could never pinpoint its origin. Once Medov returned to Russian territory, Phillips had to depend on the U.S. spy satellite, which only led to a home outside Moscow that was owned by the government, no name attached. A dead end.

But after the Capitol attack, the information found on Medov's cell phone had led to Glen Pavlov and Alex Vadin, two former high-level Russian government leaders who were giving Medov his orders.

The FBI tried to find a link from Pavlov's group to the Kremlin but came up empty.

Once Phillips' team had all of the facts and solid evidence, he met with President Fallon during the first week of August, to provide him with a full briefing on everything that had taken place. Fallon was not pleased to hear who had been behind the attack on the White House, Supreme Court and Capitol Building, but he wasn't surprised.

This was a serious enemy attack on the country, and the Russians were behind it.

He called an emergency meeting in the Situation Room with the Defense Secretary, Secretary of State, FBI, CIA and the top generals from each branch of the military. He wanted to explore all of his options, including a retaliatory strike on Moscow. After a great deal of debate and disagreement, it was decided that they would treat Pavlov and Vadin as criminals and demand that President Nikita

Patin turn them over. This avoided a major war but would be highly embarrassing for the Russians.

A five-minute phone call with President Patin was all the time it took to get that agreement. As part of the deal, Fallon could choose one media outlet to cover the arrest. This was the biggest point of contention with Patin, who didn't want any news organizations covering the arrest.

That was a deal-breaker for Fallon, a fact that quickly became clear to the Russian president, who then offered to have Channel One Russia cover it and pass along the report. Fallon actually laughed out loud at the suggestion, which Patin didn't appreciate.

"We are going to have Chet Phare from USA News cover the arrest," President Fallon told Patin in no uncertain terms. "He's the best journalist in America and will provide an honest account of the arrest."

Patin finally agreed, knowing the arrests would gain worldwide coverage and damage his reputation with the Russian people. He didn't believe he had any other good options, unless he wanted to go to war with the United States, which he knew for certain would end his long tenure as president.

The next day, a team of FBI agents arrived in Moscow. Agent Jamal Gage was given the honor of leading the SWAT Tactical Team to make the high-profile arrest. All ten men on the team were briefed and ready for anything, knowing that the Russians would be aware of their fates once they were taken into custody.

USA News planned to broadcast the major news event live, expecting every other media outlet in the world to pick up the coverage, placing the USA logo at the bottom of the screen. Executives at the network knew the live broadcast of the arrests would be an historical moment that would be replayed for decades into the future. But they also knew it would be a very dangerous moment for Phare and his crew.

Agent Gage and his FBI SWAT Tactical Team, dressed in full military gear, were driven in a large green van to a home outside

Moscow, where Gage was told he would find the two men. This was the same home Phillips had been monitoring via satellite, watching Medov enter many times.

Phillips had been told by his Russian counterpart, Savva Hachewskin, that Pavlov and Vadin had attempted to escape the country after the failed Capitol attack. However, Hachewskin claimed he had stopped them and had them held in the home, with the Russian military guarding the perimeter. Hachewskin also assured the FBI Director that all guns in the home had been confiscated.

"He must think we're stupid!" Phillips remarked to President Fallon, the morning they received that information. "Our men will go in wearing full gear, expecting them to be armed."

When Gage arrived, the Russian soldiers led him to the front door but had orders to stay outside and not be involved in any way. Gage was assured Pavlov and Vadin were inside. After quickly checking back with Phillips about the situation, he was told to go in with guns drawn.

"It's most likely a setup," Phillips told him. "Imagine the world's reaction if those two Russians shoot their way out and kill FBI agents on live TV. That would make us look bad once again. That's not going to happen!"

"I understand, sir," said Gage, a great college athlete who held the fastest time on his college football team and would most certainly be ready for anything that came his way.

USA NEWS anchor Chet Phare and his crew were apprised of the dangers but chose to follow Gage's team, determined to broadcast the moment live. In Phare's mind, even if he was shot and killed, it was an historical journalism moment that couldn't be passed up.

Gage took point, going in the front door with his Colt M4 Carbine pointed straight ahead. Four agents were right behind him, with M4 Carbines and Glock 17 handguns. Four others in the unit had gone around to the back to cut off any escape.

"FBI!" Gage announced, his voice filling the great room with high ceilings, a fan twirling overhead. "By the power of the United States of America, you are under arrest. Come out with your hands up."

Silence.

"Last chance. Come out with your hands up, or we are coming in," Gage informed loudly. Then, he checked with the team in the back. "Ready?"

"Ready!"

Gage and his men walked through the house slowly, guns pointed straight ahead, carefully checking each room. Then, they heard a loud noise from upstairs. Gage led them up the steps, with Chet Phare's cameraman, dressed in bulletproof vest and helmet, ten feet behind them.

Standing to the side of the large oak double doors of the room, Gage could easily hear someone talking, an argument.

"FBI! Open the door!" he yelled.

All of a sudden, the sound of a semiautomatic weapon was heard, bullets flying through the door, ripping into the far wall. The USA News cameraman got down on the floor, holding his camera upwards, still capturing Gage at the side of the door.

Then, with the speed that had earned him the distinction of being the fastest running back on the football team, Gage busted through the door, his rifle blazing. He dove behind a desk as fire was returned. His four men followed, firing, then ducking in, one at a time.

They took cover behind desks, bookshelves, anything to avoid being shot. One FBI agent was hit in the shoulder and jolted back. Phare's cameraman broadcast it live to the world.

A gasp could be heard from coast to coast.

Gage spotted the two Russians, one hiding inside the doorway of a closet, the other under a large desk. He watched the man in the doorway peer out, blam! Right between the eyes. Dead!

Upon seeing this, the man under the desk panicked, stood and opened up on Gage.

Outside the window, Gage could see a member of his team coming down a rope. Glock in hand, he fired at the Russian behind the desk. The Russian turned and returned fire, missing the FBI agent. But the lone rogue had now exposed himself.

Five Colt M4 Carbines inside the room fired, pelting the lone Russian criminal with dozens of bullets. Gage watched his body shake rapidly from the barrage of shots, blood spurting from his mouth, the rogue falling to the red carpet floor. Dead!

Gage ran over to check the two men bleeding on the floor. He placed two fingers on their necks one at a time. No pulse. They were dead.

The USA News cameraman was now standing, and he walked into the room, broadcasting the full bloody scene to America. It was quite a sight, to be sure. Dozens of bullet holes had torn up the once-beautiful wooden bookshelves, large desk and walls of the office. It most definitely looked like a battle zone.

Both Pavlov and Vadin lay dead on the floor, which was most likely what they would have preferred, knowing that they would receive the death sentence in America.

Chet Phare entered the room with his producer and described the scene in detail. He then approached agent Gage, who had strict instructions not to comment on anything that occurred during the arrest.

"You were told—we were all told—that these men were not armed," said Phare, who had been warned ahead of time about the strong likelihood that the men would be armed. "Do you believe that the Russians—President Patin—was trying to set you up for a disaster, an embarrassment?"

Gage just looked at the man believed to be the most honest and fair-minded journalist in the country. "That's a good question," he said, providing no further comment. "Excuse me. I need to check on my wounded man over here.

Phare went on to provide many details about the entire scene, including the fact that he had been warned ahead of time that they would probably be armed. As expected, the broadcast was picked up on television news stations across the world, except for in Russia.

CHAPTER THIRTY

The day after the attack on the Capitol Building, television news stations around the world reported on the devastating event, stating that it had been an effort by right wing militant groups. Footage of the bikers waving American flags and singing "God Bless America" were run over and over, trying to make it look like patriotic Americans were the villains—which had been Medov's plan all along.

President Fallon knew better but would wait for the right moment to prove them wrong. That moment came only a week later, when the FBI went into Moscow to arrest the two former Russian leaders who had planned all of the attacks.

With USA News providing a live report, the others in the mainstream news media who had severely criticized President Fallon and misreported the Washington attacks now sat in their newsrooms with egg on their faces, trying to back-pedal their statements and reporting. After seeing what had happened, only those on the far left continued to believe them. Their ratings plunged.

President Fallon knew the time had come to schedule an address to the nation and set the record straight.

"The men who perpetrated the attack on the U.S. Capitol and the White House in May were not patriotic Americans, as has been reported extensively by many in the news media," he began in a strong, confident tone from the newly repaired Oval Office, looking directly into the camera. "Anyone who watched the USA News coverage of the FBI's attempted arrest of the two Russians knows that for certain, since you watched it with your own eyes.

"The FBI has now compiled all of the information, leaving no doubt that this was all orchestrated by a group of Russian extremists, dating back several years. Our top FBI and CIA agents will continue to research this entire situation to find out if there is any real evidence that the Kremlin was involved. Currently, we don't have it.

"What we do know is that Glen Pavlov, the former Russian Minister of Propaganda, and Alex Vadin, the former Russian Deputy Minister of Communications, developed a strategy to take down America. We believe both men became angry when cut from their high positions in the government by President Nikita Patin.

"We believe shortly afterwards, they hatched their plan. They sent longtime KGB assassin Dmitri Medov to the United States to recruit Democratic socialist protestors, knowing they would be most eager to bring down the country.

"And they were right. Medov was able to create and infiltrate peaceful protest groups, turning them violent, as we all witnessed in Chicago, Portland, St. Louis, Kenosha and many other cities across the country.

"Medov was able to identify violent activists in our country and implement well-planned attacks, one of which took place here at the White House in June. He even brought in hired killers, men he had worked with in the past, to attack the Catholic Church in Florida and then again here in Washington, at the Cathedral of St. Matthew the Apostle.

"Dmitri Medov was a vicious Russian killer with a long record of assassinations. He was easily able to leverage the energy of socialists in this country, who thought they were doing the right thing. It doesn't take much to throw a protest into chaos and create violence. Medov was an expert, knowing all the tricks of the trade.

"Here in Washington, this past week, he brought in his lead protestors from Chicago, Jeffrey Wooten and Tim Kamus, to plan the attack on the U.S. Capitol. They were fully funded by socialist political advocate George Sorosky and also had the powerful backing of Senator Lenny Thompson. In the coming days, Attorney General Edward Crandall will be putting both Sorosky and Landers on trial for treason.

"It was their funding and support that allowed Medov and Wooten to bring in an army of violent socialists, angry leftists who were willing to kill and die for the sole purpose of bringing down America! Bringing down democracy! Destroying all of your freedoms!

"The plan included the protestors and bikers posing as loyal Americans, waving flags and singing 'God Bless America,' trying to trick the Washington Police into thinking they were patriotic citizens and not a threat. Well, they didn't fool the police, but they certainly fooled many in the news media, who swallowed the fake patriotism hook, line and sinker.

"Medov knew the success of the plan depended on total surprise, which was the purpose of that patriotic charade.

"Unfortunately for them, but fortunately for us, their plans were discovered a in a coffee shop in Chicago, by a Captain Panozzo, who passed that information along to FBI Director Sheldon Phillips and Secret Service Director Ken Hack. At that point, the FBI, Secret Service and National Guard organized their defensive plans a full two weeks before the protests were to take place.

"And you all know what happened. Our National Guard soldiers, SWAT teams, FBI agents, Secret Service and Washington Police all fought courageously to protect our nation's capital.

"We lost thirty-five brave men and women in the battle. We have posted their names on the White House website and will be meeting with their families this week. We can't express enough our great appreciation for their true dedication, true patriotism and sacrifice for our country.

"In addition, as you know from the extensive news reports, the Speaker of the House, Fritzi Bello, and Senate Minority Whip, Calvin Huster, were killed by Medov, point-blank, in the Capitol Building. Our condolences go out to their families, whom I will also be meeting with this week. Both will be honored, lying in state in the Capitol Rotunda, on Tuesday of this week, with funerals on Wednesday and Thursday.

"Finally, I would like to call on all Americans to please use this terrible experience as a lesson of understanding that we all live in the greatest country in the history of the world. In that position, there will always be evil-minded people both within the country and outside our borders seeking to bring us down. They have created misinformation campaigns, implemented through the traditional news media and social media, which have influenced some of you to turn against your country. They are smart, clever adversaries. They use the anger and hate in some of our citizens, and their freedom to express it, and try to turn it against all Americans.

"That's why tonight, I am announcing the assembly of a News Standards and Practices Committee, comprised of experts in journalism, law, history and government.

"My fellow Americans, we have to set a standard, a bar whereby any news organization, including social media, will be held to reporting the facts or they won't be allowed to report the news any longer.

"I know that sounds like a tricky proposition. And it is. But we have to eliminate the misinformation that is reported to Americans on a daily basis. It's now a danger to our country. I'm confident the right group of experts can develop the standards and practices needed to achieve that very important objective and still keep our freedom of speech intact, with a contingency of responsible speech by the news media now attached.

"Thank you all for your time. And God bless America!"

As could be expected, President Fallon's speech was ripped royally by the talking heads on most mainstream media outlets, but especially on CBN and LNN. He just smiled as he watched them, knowing their days of spewing poisonous misinformation across the country would soon come to an end.

The next evening, a few miles away, Ken and Elizabeth Hack

hosted a party for all of those who had led the fight against the Russians and violent socialists. Standing in the Hacks' living room sipping champagne were FBI Director Sheldon Phillips and agent Jamal Gage, National Guard General Jerry Lewandowski, FBI SWAT Commander Dirk Williams, Air Traffic Controller Alfred Soldatz, Navy Pilot Ben Stevens and Agent Denny Perme.

They were all surrounding Dylan Reilly, who was introducing them to Captain Panozzo, Marty Mahoney, and Kiki Krup, all of whom had played such a key role in thwarting the attack on Washington. Dylan also used the opportunity to personally thank each and every one of those men and women for their courage in the line of fire.

As Ken Hack lifted his glass to toast Alfred Soldatz and Ben Stevens for shooting those planes out of the sky, a surprise guest appeared at the front door. President Fallon and his wife Carol entered with Attorney General Crandell and Secret Service Agent James Hicks.

President Fallon received a very warm reception from the entire group, who sincerely appreciated his efforts to defend the country under such trying times.

"A toast to our beloved President," said Ken Hack, holding his champagne glass high. "Here's to a man who will always do the right thing to protect the freedoms of our country, even when he knows he will be heavily criticized by some in the news media."

"Hear, hear!" was voiced at once by all in the room.

A few moments later, it seemed everyone wanted to personally ask Hicks about the moment that had made him famous, pulling the number-one terrorist in the world out of the hole in the ground in Iraq. He smiled, having told the story a million times. But for this group, a million-one would be an honor, he thought.

"And let me just say to all of you," Hicks said, holding up a glass of champagne, "Hopefully this battle will help some of those who have been brainwashed against America to learn a little more about their country, a little more about the men and women who have fought and died for their freedoms, a little more about the great privilege it is to live in the United States. God bless America!"

"God bless America!" they all said in unison with glasses raised, then sipping sweet freedom, a taste never to be underappreciated.

CHAPTER THIRTY-ONE

Praying on the old creaky red kneelers, with head down on prayerful hands pointed toward the cross of Christ high above at St. Peter's Catholic Church, Dylan Reilly had so much to be thankful for on this bright, sunny Sunday morning. He had once again survived a vicious battle, this one bigger and more dangerous than any gunfight in the past.

He thanked God for allowing him to live to continue his mission but prayed for all of the courageous soldiers and SWAT officers who had died defending their country on that fateful morning in Washington, which was now being called Bloody Saturday.

Ending the lives of one hundred and twenty-six enemy combatants, protestors and bikers, could not be taken lightly. He hated the thought of it but knew it was all carried out in Just Defense.

Somehow, it didn't feel the same as the days when he had stopped the Al-Qaeda terrorists at the Midwest Trade Building, or bank robbers, or white supremacists at the community rally.

This was different. With the exception of Medov, Wooten, Kamus, and Slagle, Dylan believed most of the men and women who had joined the socialist uprising to attack the U.S. Capitol were just thoroughly confused, brain-washed into believing they were doing the right thing.

How he wished he could have had each of them in his history classroom, to teach them about the 1917 revolution in Russia and how poorly the communist party in the Soviet Union had treated the Russian people! It wasn't Haight-Ashbury and the Summer of Love, although Dylan knew that even that historical moment in San Francisco had been horribly misrepresented. The peace, love and communal sharing mindset the hippies and yippies had started in

June of the summer of 1967 only lasted a few months before drugs, rape and theft ruined the "Flower Children's" party.

Dylan finished his prayers with a plea to God for all Americans to read history and learn from the experiences of those who had come before them so there could be a reference to the knowledge gained from those times in order to make the best present-day decisions. He knew that was a lot to ask, and a pipe dream, but he also knew that with God, all things were possible.

Dylan watched his good friend, Father Patrick Quilty, lead the 10 o'clock mass, but regrettably could not accept communion from the priest he respected so much. That would have to wait until he could return to the state of grace following confession.

"The mass is ended. Go in peace," said Father Quilty, concluding the mass and walking down the steps back to the sacristy. Dylan made the sign of the cross, stood and walked to the west wall of the church, entering the now-very-familiar confessional.

"Bless me, Father, for I have sinned," said the devout Catholic, eager to cleanse his soul. "My last confession was three weeks ago."

CHAPTER THIRTY-TWO

Leaving St. Peter's Church that Sunday morning, Dylan was curious about the man who had asked to meet him at the intersection of LaSalle and Jackson, near the Midwest Trade Building, where he had stopped the terrorist attack a year earlier.

This man had contacted Father Quilty but wouldn't give him his name. A red flag, to be sure, but the always-helpful priest had still passed the message along to Dylan.

"I'm sorry you have suddenly become the intermediary for people trying to contact me," Dylan expressed to his friend at the back of the church, after finishing his penance prayers. "I don't understand why they don't just approach me after mass. Anyway, hopefully it won't happen again. Sorry, Father."

Smiles. Nods. A handshake and goodbyes.

As Dylan walked west down Madison toward LaSalle on this sunny Sunday morning, he was, as always, so amazed at the empty streets of downtown, which would come to life the next morning. At the intersection of Madison and LaSalle stood a homeless man holding a cup. Dylan pulled the wallet from his coat, opened it and handed the man a $5 McDonald's gift card and wished him well.

The man smiled and thanked him. No money for booze, but a free meal. Great!

Dylan turned left down LaSalle Street, and with so few cars on the four-lane road, Dylan could easily see the Midwest Trade Building, four blocks north. Crossing Monroe, he noticed white trailers and large trucks parked on both sides of the street. Dylan, like most Chicagoans, knew that meant a movie or TV show was shooting there. Chicago had become a prime destination for Hollywood, due to the impressive skyline and landscape, as well as its location and wealth of available acting and production talent.

As he strolled down LaSalle, past the long white tractor trailers used for the film company's equipment, parked between Adams and Jackson, he saw a sign that read, "Who's the Best?"

Uh-oh, he thought. What is this all about? Then, he saw that LaSalle Street was completely empty, past the barricades set across the entire intersection. Dozens of young college-aged students were lined up behind the blue wooden horse blockades that read "Chicago Police—Do Not Cross."

Obviously, everyone was there to see the filming. All eyes were focused on a cowboy standing in the middle of an empty LaSalle Street. He was a fairly tall, tough-looking, unshaven man in a black cowboy hat. No question he had to be the star of the show.

Two camera crews were positioned to film the cowboy, one in front of him and the other to his right.

Dylan immediately thought Father Quilty must have made a mistake about the location. They were shooting a movie, which looked to be some type of western.

Oh, well. Mistakes happened. But since he was there, Dylan thought he would watch them film the scene. This was his first time watching a movie being shot, so he was pretty excited and curious about the entire process.

He walked up to a small opening along the barricade, between two young men in colorful t-shirts and jeans. That seemed to be the dress code for nearly all the young people that morning.

"Hi, fellows," Dylan said to be friendly, then wedged himself between them. "What movie are they shooting?"

They both looked at him. Jaws dropped. Dylan knew what was coming. "You're the guy!" said the curly brown-haired boy on his left, then turned to his pal. "Hey, he's the guy!"

Murmurs grew throughout the crowd, pointing, heads turning, whispers. Dylan had become used to it, but never welcomed the attention.

"Yeah, I can see that, Derrick," replied his blond-haired friend, sporting the pompadour cut of the day. "It's not a movie, sir. It's a reality TV show."

Dylan nodded, somewhat surprised. A fake cowboy standing in the middle of LaSalle Street. Where was the reality in that, he wondered.

Then, he looked out at the cowboy, who just stood there, staring straight ahead. He certainly looked the part of a cowboy, Dylan thought, with the large black hat, tan Legacy Drifter coat and high leather boots.

Dylan then watched a man to the side of the cowboy walk up to him. He was pointing toward Adams, looking like he was giving him instructions. He must have been the director, Dylan thought. Then, he watched the cowboy pull his coat back, revealing a Smith and Wesson six-shooter in a dark brown holster. Dylan smiled. Perhaps he had started a trend that was now being used in TV shows and movies, he thought.

"What are you smiling for?" the cowboy said loudly, for all to hear.

This was exciting, Dylan thought. They were starting the scene.

Then, the cowboy took a few steps forward. He seemed to be looking directly at Dylan, who turned around to see if there was something behind him that was in the shot.

No, nothing there.

Then, all of the college guys lined up along the barricades picked up the two wooden horses in front of Dylan and moved them onto the sidewalk.

Everyone who had been lined up behind them began moving to the west side of the street, so Dylan turned to follow them.

"I'm talking to you, Mr. Fastest Gun!" barked out the cowboy, and one of the camera men swung around, his large zoom lens pointing directly at Dylan, the only one left in the middle of the street, just twenty-five yards from the cowboy.

Silence. The sound of the el train rumbling in the background.

And there they stood, the tough cowboy and Dylan Reilly, twenty-five yards apart, with dozens of onlookers watching from the sidewalks.

Dylan now understood that he had been set up. He hadn't been asked to be in a reality show, so he wasn't sure why they were filming him being challenged by a reality show cowboy.

"I watched you in Grant Park last year, when everyone was cheering for… The Fastest Gun!" the cowboy emphatically blurted out, leaving no question about whom he was talking to. "Well, mister, you aren't so fast. But you're looking at the fastest gun. And I'm here to prove it to you."

The sidewalk spectators all turned toward America's hero. What would he do?

Dylan was dumbstruck, having no idea how to react to this ridiculous challenge. He looked around, then toward the man he thought was the director, who was just standing there, wearing an old blue baseball cap, watching his unrehearsed scene play out.

"What are you looking for, your momma?" said the tough-looking cowboy in a low, gravelly voice.

Murmurs. Wide eyes.

"Can someone tell me what's going on here?" Dylan called out, looking at the camera person filming him. "Mister Director? What's the deal here?"

"What's wrong, Dylan Reilly? You yellow?"

Loud murmurs from both sides of the street. Eyes wider. Mouths agape. Whispers of, "He just called him yellow."

"Look, mister, what do you want from me?" Dylan asked in a not-so-friendly tone, completely annoyed and out of patience, coming off of the battle in Washington.

"A duel!" barked the man. "Let's find out right now who is the fastest gun."

Silence. All heads turn to Dylan.

"I don't want to kill you, mister," Dylan grimaced.

"Kill me?" the cowboy laughed. "Oh, I don't think you're going to have to worry about that, sonny."

Dylan watched the cowboy take a few strides closer. "Now, I'm going to give you to the count of three to step out here and face me like a man."

"Or what? What are you going to do, tough guy?" Dylan barked back, now more than a little angry about what was taking place. The director smiling wide. This was better than anything he had imaged. The audience enjoying every second of the confrontation.

"Or I'll just have to shoot you like the coward you are," said the cowboy.

Oooooh! Rang across LaSalle.

Well, that was all the pushing Dylan was going to take from the ugly cowboy with the big nose and elephant ears. If he wanted a gunfight, a gunfight he would get. And now America's hero was more than a little irritated. So maybe he wouldn't be as nice to this cowboy as he had been to Senator Thompson, just shooting the musket out of his hand, not killing him.

Dylan stepped forward into the middle of LaSalle. He was now only twenty feet from the cowboy.

Along the sidewalks, the mouths of spectators became dry. Eyes grew wide. The director watched intently. This was a real gunfight, just like in the old west. Gary Cooper in *High Noon*. Clint Eastwood in *The Good, The Bad and The Ugly*. Kevin Costner in *Open Range*.

This was cool! But someone was going to lose. Would someone die right there on LaSalle? Would this be the end of America's hero? Or would the reality star cowboy have his fifteen minutes of fame cut short?

Those thoughts passed through the hearts and minds of the sixty college-aged students standing on the sidewalk on both sides of LaSalle. All the young men and women were extras, hired to give their real reaction to this new reality show, *Who's the Best?* hosted by Tony Danza, former star of *Who's the Boss?*

Dylan stood and pulled back the right side of his coat, revealing his famed silver six-shooter, shining bright from the sun showing through the downtown skyscrapers.

The crowd gasped at the sight of it, having seen it on news reports so many times. Now, they were staring at the real thing. Exciting!

"Okay, well, I see you're ready to meet your maker," the cowboy threatened, sounding like he had spent his Saturday mornings watching one too many westerns on Turner Classic Movies.

The two men stared at each other, waiting for one to make the first move. Dylan knew the drill. He had been trained so well by Sergeant Henry. It wasn't the man's hand he would be watching. It was his eyes.

His face and eyes would tell him when his opponent would draw. It had worked for him a year earlier, when he had stood face to face with the two Al-Qaeda terrorists holding their semiautomatic weapons on him. It was all in the eyes. He had known exactly when that terrorist was going to squeeze that trigger. And with lightning-fast speed had shot him, before the terrorist could do it.

This face-off was easier. The cowboy would have to actually draw his gun from his holster.

Quiet fell over LaSalle Street. The el train could be heard rumbling over the tracks a few blocks south, pulling into the Van Buren Station.

Dylan watched the cowboy's eyes. They narrowed a bit. Then, his cheeks moved. That was it. The cowboy's right hand came up fast to grab his gun. But not fast enough. Not even close.

Dylan—with incredible speed, lightning-fast quickness, faster than he had ever drawn—drew his gun and blam! Shot the six-shooter right out of the cowboy's hand. The now-damaged silver gun sailed in the air, landing four feet behind the very embarrassed cowpoke, who looked at his gun on the ground then back at Dylan.

All eyes watched the cowboy.

His eyes kept telling the story. Dylan knew he wasn't finished.

When guys were beat, their energy dropped. This man's energy was still high.

"Well, I guess you beat me, eh?" said the cowboy, smiling and nodding, then turning toward the crowd of extras on the sidewalk to his left. "So I guess that's it, huh, folks? I guess Dylan Reilly is the fastest gun, eh?"

Dylan kept watching him. The cowboy's eyes narrowed again.

Then, very quickly, the cowboy jerked his right arm forward, and a gray Glock gun appeared from inside the sleeve of his Legacy Drifter and then in his hand.

The crowd screamed, totally surprised.

Dylan, unfazed, drew his gun again, and blam!

The Glock went spinning off into the air. Then, blam! A silver bullet right into the man's upper right thigh. The cowboy bent over, grabbed his thigh and fell backward to the ground, his thick Legacy Drifter helping to break his fall.

Dylan hadn't wanted to hurt the cowboy, but the cowboy had given him no choice. At least Dylan had let him live, using Ken Hack's recommendation for stopping an attacker without killing them. Hack had done it in D.C. and now Dylan on LaSalle Street.

It was over. The director was now visibly shaken. The reality of his reality show suddenly dawned on him. Someone had actually gotten hurt.

The college kids stood in awe of what they had just witnessed. The sheer speed of Dylan Reilly! So fast, he could shoot the gun out of the cowboy's hand. Then, he had done it again. Incredible!

"Wow! Did you see that?" was muttered all along LaSalle.

"Fast! So fast!" echoed through the street.

Then a few on the sidewalk started clapping. Then more. Loud applause erupted.

"Dylan! Dylan! Dylan!" the young fans sang out, having witnessed a real gunfight. Not a movie. Not a TV show. But a real gunfight

"So cool! Incredible! Totally fun!" they would recall for family and friends, anyone who would listen, for years to come.

"Except for that injured cowboy, of course," they would say. "But he had it coming. Pulling that Glock out from under his coat. That was a low-down, dirty trick. But still, Dylan stopped him. So fast!"

The cowboy was being attended to by two lady paramedics. From the pavement, he lifted himself up enough to look at Reilly, seeing the hero he had hoped to be that day. He heard the loud applause and chants that he had hoped to receive that morning. Depressed by the scene, he lay flat on his back again.

"Is he going to be okay?" Dylan asked the paramedic with the long black ponytail, who looked up and flashed a bright white smile.

"Oh, yeah, he's going to be just fine," she said, holding the cowboy up in her arms as the other red-haired paramedic applied large white bandages to stop the bleeding. "You put that bullet in a good spot. It will be an easy surgery to pull it out and patch it up."

Dylan nodded, then looked down at the injured man. "Sorry, cowboy. I wish I didn't have to hurt you."

The cowboy's lower lip stiffened as he looked up. "Hurt me?" he sputtered. "Hurt me? You didn't hurt me, Dylan Reilly, you no-good, low-down…"

"Oh, brother!" said Dylan, rolling his eyes. "I've got to go."

"Oh, wait, Dylan. Can I get a photo with you?" asked the pretty paramedic, dropping the cowboy back onto the pavement.

For the next twenty minutes, both paramedics, the director, the crew and every sidewalk fan took the opportunity to take a photo with their hero.

Smiles, hugs, kisses, cheers. A Sunday morning that could have been marred by an unnecessary death was a joyous celebration of fandom and friendliness. A long line formed on the street, each waiting for the iPhone moment.

As Dylan stood smiling next to the curly brown-haired college boy he had first met by the barricade that morning, the sound of the el train could be heard in the background. Thankfully, it drowned out the moaning and muttering of a fool in a cowboy hat, with his drifter lying on the gurney, being placed into the back of an ambulance.

Dylan's phone rang. Robyn's name on caller ID. "Hi, Robyn!" he said, excited to receive her call.

"Dylan, I have to meet with you," she said, her voice in a panic. "I have to tell you something that I should have told you before."

Holding his phone to his ear, his mind racing, Dylan looked up to the blue skies, wondering what was it that she hadn't told him. He would soon find out.

THE END

ABOUT THE AUTHOR

John Ruane is an author, journalist, playwright and actor. He has written for the *Chicago Sun-Times, Chicago Tribune,* and *Atlanta-Journal Constitution.* He is a critically-acclaimed author of five books, including *The Earl Campbell Story* (ECW Press, 1999) and *Parish the Thought* (Simon & Schuster, 2008). *A Dangerous Freedom* is his first thriller novel, published by Permuted Press, and the beginning of the Dylan Reilly series.

Since leaving the Sun-Times, John has made his living in the public relations industry, creating and implementing several award-winning programs. He is a graduate of Chicago State University where he was an English major, wrote a column for the school newspaper, played center on two college hockey championship teams and pitched for the Cougars baseball team. Later, he volunteered his time to coaching fifty-two youth sports teams over a 17-year period.

John and his wife, Charlotte, are proud parents of four adult children and three grandchildren.

Made in United States
Orlando, FL
08 June 2023